TEWKESBURY TOMB

A captivating Victorian historical murder mystery

KERRY TOMBS

Inspector Ravenscroft Detective Mysteries Book 4

JOFFE BOOKS

Revised edition 2020
Joffe Books, London
www.joffebooks.com

First published in Great Britain 2011

ISBN 978-1-78931-598-1

For Samuel and Zoe
— with love, for they are
the future

PROLOGUE

TEWKESBURY, MARCH 1889

'Time?'

'Thirty minutes past eleven, my dear sir.'

'Confound it!' exclaimed Mr Ganniford, pacing up and down before the roaring log fire in the snug of the Hop Pole Hotel.

'I find that time always goes at a far slower pace when one is eager for it to proceed at a greater rate,' replied his companion, removing his spectacles from his thin nose and blowing sharply upon them.

'The trouble with you, Jenkins, is that you never allow yourself the opportunity to rise to the occasion. You have spent far too many days reading uninteresting ancient historical journals in that drab little London club of yours, instead of sampling the pleasures that life presents to one,' pronounced Ganniford, throwing his bulky frame into one of the well-worn leather armchairs.

'And the trouble with you, my dear Ganniford, is that in all the years I have known you, you have never shown the slightest inclination of mastering that impatient nature of yours — and you seem content to indulge in too much over-dining at other men's tables and gambling your inheritance away at Brooks',' reprimanded the older man removing a large handkerchief from his pocket and applying it vigorously to the lens.

'Better to have lived an impatient life full of optimistic expectation than to have died after a lifetime of boredom and sobriety.'

His companion allowed himself a brief smile. 'Caution and moderation in all things, Ganniford — caution and moderation.'

'Nonsense, my dear fellow, you need to push aside your ancient dusty books and indulge yourself more.'

'Human life is everywhere in a state where much is to be endured, and little to be enjoyed.'

'And I suppose that was said by one of your ancient Greeks?'

'Samuel Johnson, actually.'

'You made sure you paid that man to meet us there?' said the other, ignoring the last remark and changing the subject.

'At twelve, as agreed, outside the main entrance.'

'I suppose he will be there?'

'If the fellow wants a further ten shillings,' replied Jenkins, lifting up his spectacles at arm's length so that the light from the fire was reflected in the glass.

'You think there may be others?' asked the other anxiously.

'The letter did not imply that there would be.'

'But there must be others. He had seemed to indicate that there would be others?'

'I do not know whether there will be anyone else there tonight, or not,' said Jenkins, with a note of indifference as he replaced his spectacles on the end of his nose.

'Bound to be others. Can't see how it could be otherwise,' muttered Ganniford before taking another sip of his ale.

The older man shrugged his shoulders and stared into the flames.

'What do you make of the town?' asked his companion after a few moments of silence.

'It appears to have some fine buildings, although I must admit that I could see little from our cab as we entered the place.'

'Dull, provincial little backwater!' exclaimed Ganniford shifting about uneasily in his armchair.

'Rather a rash, and no doubt, unfounded conclusion, if I may say so. You have spent far too much of your time in London. There is another world you know, my dear Ganniford, which lies outside the confines of the metropolis, waiting to be discovered.'

'Then it can be savoured by others. That is rich coming from a man who has spent a lifetime in dusty libraries. As soon as this business has been bought to a satisfactory conclusion, I will be more than pleased to return to the pleasures of the great city, at the earliest opportunity,' protested Ganniford, before taking another drink from his tumbler.

'As you wish.'

'And why you would insist on stopping off at Oxford for the day, when we could have come directly here by express train, I shall never know.'

'I thought you might have appreciated the opportunity of visiting the university town to view the college buildings. There were one or two artefacts I wished to see at the Ashmolean,' replied Jenkins, leaning forward and moving one of the logs in the hearth with the brass poker.

His companion said nothing as he rose from his chair and walked over to the window.

'I suppose your room is not to your liking?' asked Jenkins, regretting the words as soon as he had uttered them.

'Dull, my dear sir! Dull beyond description. Drab curtains, decaying wooden furniture, cracked wash bowl, uncomfortable bed, horrible wallpaper, dreadful coloured bedspread, and the smell of onions and decay everywhere! I hardly know where to begin. But I suppose that is what one must expect in such a town as this.'

‘I am sorry for it.’

‘I’m afraid we shall not have a good night for it. I believe the rain has not ceased since our arrival, and shows little promise of improvement,’ sighed Ganniford, pulling a long face before returning to the hearth and standing once more before the flames. ‘What shall we say, Jenkins, if anyone enquires as to the nature of our business here?’

‘We shall say we are pilgrims.’

‘Pilgrims?’ asked the younger man.

‘Pilgrims, come to see the holy relics in the abbey.’

‘What holy relics?’

‘The Duke of Clarence and his wife.’

‘And who precisely was Clarence?’

‘The Duke of Clarence was the younger brother of King Edward IV, and elder brother of King Richard III. He is believed to have drowned in a butt of malmsey,’ said Jenkins, adopting that dry matter-of-fact tone which his companion had long been acquainted with.

‘That sounds a most interesting, but unfortunate way to die, implying a degree of carelessness on his part. You must tell me more when we are faced with an evening when we have little else to entertain us. Anyway, I thought that people did not go on pilgrimages any more these days.’

‘Far from it, my dear Ganniford. Many people visit Canterbury each year in remembrance of Thomas Becket, and some more adventurous souls still undertake the arduous journey to Santiago de Compostela in northern Spain to see the shrine there dedicated to St James.’

‘Whatever for?’ inquired Ganniford, regaining his seat before the fire.

‘The pilgrims believe that by undertaking such a journey their sins will be cleansed. Some are also afflicted by various ailments and hope that they may be cured.’

‘And are they?’

‘I believe that in some cases they are, although I must say I have never had the first-hand experience of witnessing any such miraculous cure.’

'Hum. Stuff and nonsense! People often believe what they want to believe.'

'We live in an enlightened age, Ganniford, and as such must be open to all possibilities and suggestions. It is only a closed mind which fears that which it cannot understand,' said Jenkins leaning forward and warming his hands in front of the flames.

'If I had closed my mind, I would not have been sitting here tonight in this draughty old inn in this dreary old town, waiting for the time to approach twelve o'clock, so that I could enter a cold uninviting abbey looking for the grave of this old Templar fellow of yours,' muttered Ganniford.

'Ah, but the promise of what such a visit may yield, you must find intriguing to say the least.'

'That remains to be seen.'

'Excuse me, gentlemen, for intruding upon your conversation.'

Startled by the words, the two men turned round to see who the voice belonged to, and were surprised to find a middle-aged lady dressed in a plain beige coloured coat and bonnet standing before them. 'I'm sorry, I did not mean to startle you.'

'Not at all, my dear lady,' replied Ganniford, as he and his companion started to rise from their armchairs.

'I could not help hearing part of your earlier conversation, gentlemen, seated as I was around the corner. I believe we may share the same common purpose tonight.'

'I told you there would be others, Jenkins!' exclaimed Ganniford, feeling the satisfaction that his premise had proven true.

'You must forgive my colleague's over enthusiasm. Allow me to introduce myself, Thomas Jenkins, antiquarian and scholar of London — and this is my companion, Mr Nathaniel Ganniford,' said the older gentleman giving a short bow in the stranger's direction.

'Gentlemen. My name is Miss Eames, from Ludlow.'

'Eames. The name seems familiar, but I cannot place it at the present. So you, too, have travelled far to be here tonight, Miss Eames,' said Ganniford smiling.

'Yes indeed, gentlemen.'

'Your journey must have been arduous?' enquired Jenkins.

'I broke my journey at Hereford yesterday evening, before travelling onward today. The train was rather slow.'

'I have heard good things about Ludlow, Miss Eames,' continued Jenkins, indicating that the new arrival should accept his place before the fire.

'No, thank you, I would rather stand. Ludlow is indeed a fine place. It is a pretty town with a fine castle. I have lived there all my life, with my late father who has recently died, and would want for no other.'

'I am sorry for your loss,' said the older man sympathetically.

'You are very kind, sir.'

'Look here, Jenkins, the clock must be fast approaching twelve. What say I go and secure a lantern from the landlord, so we can light our way across to the abbey? Miss Eames, perhaps you may permit us to escort you, as you also appear to have an interest in this case?' inquired Ganniford.

'That is most kind of you, gentlemen.'

* * *

A few minutes later the party closed the outer door of the Hop Pole behind them, and made their way across the street, Ganniford holding the lantern up high to aid their progress, Jenkins giving his assistance to the recent arrival. Quickly passing by the old almshouses on their right-hand side, and some school buildings on their left, the trio walked quickly up the pathway, through the falling rain, towards the ancient building that gradually came into view before them.

'It appears that we are expected,' cried out Ganniford, pointing towards a distant light which appeared to originate from the front entrance.

‘Who is there? Show yourselves!’ shouted a voice as they neared the flickering flame.

‘Three strangers intent on business,’ replied Jenkins.

‘Blazes!’ exclaimed another voice.

‘Wretched inclement weather,’ wheezed Ganniford, as he and his party hastily sought the cover of the porch.

‘I gather we are of a similar intention?’ asked Jenkins, addressing the two figures who stood before them.

‘If you mean seeking out the Templar monument, then we are indeed of a similar tendency,’ replied the figure who had first called out to them.

‘Quite. Allow me to introduce my companions — Miss Eames from Ludlow, Mr Jenkins from London, and I am Mr Ganniford, also from London, at your service, gentlemen.’

‘Doctor Andreas Hollinger, formerly of Baden-Baden,’ said the elderly, grey-haired gentleman, speaking in a pronounced foreign accent, and extending a hand in greeting.

‘Major Anstruther, Her Majesty’s Dragoon Guards at your service, gentlemen, and lady,’ added the other stranger giving a short bow.

‘Have you been here long, gentlemen?’ enquired Ganniford.

‘Only these past ten minutes,’ replied the doctor.

‘I had thought that our host would have been here to welcome us,’ said Jenkins, brushing away some of the wet from his coat.

‘Probably thought better of it,’ said the military gentleman, running a finger over a red moustache.

‘The night is certainly, how you say, it is wretched,’ remarked Hollinger smiling.

‘I took the liberty, gentlemen, of securing the services of a local man, who, I assume, is the custodian of the building. He declared he would be here tonight to unlock the door for us,’ said Jenkins, in his usual matter-of-fact tone of voice.

‘Then it would appear, sir, that the fellow ran off with your money!’ snapped Anstruther striding up and down.

'We are a few minutes early, I believe,' said his companion pulling out a large watch from his waistcoat pocket and examining its hands.

'Good evening, gentlemen!'

The group turned round to discover that a tall, thin gentleman, dressed in a long black coat and slouch hat, had suddenly entered the porch.

'And who the devil are you?' asked Anstruther.

'Ross. My name is Ross, gentlemen. At your service. I'm sorry, ma'am, I did not observe your presence,' said the new arrival addressing Miss Eames.

'I take it, sir, that you are engaged on the same business as ourselves?' asked Ganniford after clearing his throat, and observing that the speaker had a marked Scottish accent and that his face was partially obscured by his large hat.

'I believe so, gentlemen.'

'Your voice suggests that you have, how you say, travelled far?' said Hollinger.

'I originate from Kirkintilloch, gentlemen, in Dumbartonshire, but now reside near Bredon,' replied Ross, in a formal, brisk tone that suggested that he was unwilling to engage in further conversation.

'Then you have had the shortest journey of all of us,' said Jenkins, giving the stranger a curious stare.

The latest arrival said nothing, as he turned away from the group.

'Damn cold out here tonight,' said the major, stamping his feet on the ground.

'Miss Eames — and gentlemen, as it would appear that neither our host, nor the person you engaged, Mr Jenkins, is here tonight to, er, meet us, then perhaps we should adjourn to one of the nearby inns, and return in, say, thirty minutes' time?' suggested the doctor.

'You can go to the inn if you want to, I will remain here,' retorted Anstruther. 'I've come a damn long way to be here tonight, and I'm not inclined to forsake our quest now.'

'I was not implying that we abandon our visit entirely, Major. I was merely suggesting that we return later. I'm sure Miss Eames must be feeling the cold,' corrected Hollinger becoming somewhat flushed in the face.

'I agree with the major. If we go away now, and if either our host or this fellow you have engaged, Jenkins, was to turn up in our absence and see we were not here, he might decide not to wait for our return,' offered Ganniford.

'I am quite content to remain here, gentlemen,' said Miss Eames, before Hollinger could reply.

'Then it is agreed, we shall all remain,' added Jenkins, observing that during this conversation Ross had moved across towards the large oak door and had been busily intent on turning its iron handle.

'My word, Ross, I do believe that you have found the door to be open!' exclaimed Ganniford.

The Scotsman said nothing as he stepped into the building.

'Well that is fortunate indeed. I think we should follow Mr Ross, gentlemen. After you, my good lady,' said Hollinger.

One by one the group entered the Abbey.

'Hold the lantern up, Ganniford,' instructed Jenkins trying to adjust his eyes to the intense darkness of the interior.

'Hello! Hello! Is there anyone here?' shouted out his companion, complying with the request.

'It would appear that we are, how you say, not with others, but quite alone, gentlemen,' said Hollinger, raising the other lantern.

'Perhaps we should withdraw, gentlemen, and return in the morning,' suggested Miss Eames.

'Unsporting of our host not to be here to great us, after the long way we have all come,' muttered Anstruther, ignoring the last remark. 'Bad manners I call it, and damned inconvenient.'

'What are we to do now, gentlemen?' asked Hollinger, a worried expression on his face.

'I must confess I am at a loss as to how to proceed,' said Jenkins.

'Look here, in the letter it said something about the old knight's tomb, or monument, or something like that,' said Ganniford.

'Ah, Sir Roger de la Pole, I believe that was his name. He is one of your Templar Knights buried here in the abbey,' offered Hollinger.

'Well if we find the tomb then perhaps we would then know how next to proceed,' said Ganniford, becoming increasingly impatient.

'Capital idea! Rather dark in here though,' said Major Anstruther.

'It is rather a large building, gentlemen,' said Miss Eames.

'Would do no harm to look,' urged Ganniford.

'May I make a suggestion?' said Jenkins. 'As we are six in number, and yet have only two lanterns, why do we not form two groups and divide the lanterns between us. Ganniford and Miss Eames shall accompany me down the left-hand side of the abbey, whilst you Hollinger, Major and Ross take the other side.'

'Excellent suggestion, sir,' echoed Anstruther.

'Speaking of Mr Ross, I cannot see the gentleman,' said Hollinger.

The five members looked intently around them, straining to see any sign of their companion in the gloom.

'I don't believe I've seen him since we entered the building,' said a puzzled Ganniford. 'He must have begun to search the abbey by himself.'

'Then no doubt we shall shortly meet up with him again. If you would care to proceed onwards Herr Jenkins with your group, and Major if you would accompany me,' said Hollinger.

'If we find this Pole fellow first we'll give you a shout,' indicated Ganniford as they set off.

'And we will do the same,' added Hollinger.

'You keep the lantern, Ganniford. Miss Eames if you would care to take my arm, so that neither of the three of us becomes separated.'

'That is most kind of you, Mr Jenkins.'

Ganniford lead the way cautiously down the side aisle of the building, holding the lantern in front of the group, and pausing now and then so that they could examine the various monuments that lay along the side of the wall, and occasionally glancing across at the other party's lantern as it flickered in the darkness.

'It would help if I knew what we were looking for,' said Ganniford, irritably, after a few minutes had elapsed.

'I believe that Sir Roger de la Pole would be buried inside a monumental tomb of some kind,' replied Jenkins. 'It might even have his effigy on top of it.'

'Can't see who this fellow is,' said Ganniford bringing the lantern closer to one of the monuments. 'The carving's long been worn away, and there does not appear to be any lettering left round the sides.'

'I think that monument probably relates to one of the old abbots,' said the lady of their party.

'You seem remarkably well informed, Miss Eames,' said Jenkins.

'I have seen similar edifices in other religious buildings.'

'Nothing for it then but to continue our search,' sighed Ganniford.

As the trio moved deeper into the abbey, the lantern threw up enlarged shadows of themselves onto the walls of the building and, as they neared the centre, they could hear the occasional sound of footsteps in the far distance.

Suddenly a voice, whom they recognized as belonging to Hollinger, cried out in the darkness, 'Over here, gentlemen. We have found the Templar!'

'Can you hold your lantern higher so we may see you?' asked Ganniford.

'There!' pointed Miss Eames.

The three seekers quickly made their way across to the other side of the building, where Major Anstruther and Doctor Hollinger were waiting for them.

'I believe this is what we are looking for. Sir Roger de la Pole, the Templar Knight,' said Hollinger, holding the lantern high so that its rays fell on the mounted sarcophagus.

'No sign of Ross?' asked Jenkins.

'Good heavens! It looks as though someone has recently forced open the tomb!' exclaimed Anstruther. 'Bring the lantern closer.'

The group crowded round the stone monument.

'I believe you're correct, Major. It looks as though someone has opened the lid,' said Ganniford leaning forwards.

'Some effort would have been required. The stone must weigh a great deal,' added Jenkins.

'Why would someone want to break into the tomb?' asked Miss Eames.

'We may be able to look inside. Bring the light nearer, Hollinger, so that I can see,' instructed Anstruther.

'Can you see anything?' enquired Ganniford impatiently as the major peered into the sarcophagus.

'My God, there's a body in here!'

'The ancient bones of Sir Roger, I expect,' suggested Jenkins.

'No, not bones, gentlemen. Good grief, it is none other than our missing host Grantly!' exclaimed Anstruther stepping back from the tomb.

'Let me see,' said Ganniford moving forward quickly and bringing the lantern closer to the monument.

'What can you see?' asked Jenkins eagerly.

'It's Stanhope!' replied Ganniford. 'What can you see, Hollinger?'

The doctor took the lantern and stared down into the open tomb, before stepping back and addressing the group. 'Major, you said you believed the body to be that of a certain Mr Grantly?'

'Yes, Grantly,' replied the military gentleman.

'And you, Mr Ganniford, thought the man to be a Mr Stanhope?'

'Yes. He told me his name was Stanhope,' answered a bewildered Ganniford.

'Well, that is most strange, gentlemen, for you see I recognize the deceased as a Dr Thorne,' continued Hollinger.

The members of the group looked at one another for some seconds before Jenkins broke the silence. 'Perhaps I may be able to clarify the situation. If you will allow me the lantern for a moment, my dear Ganniford?'

Jenkins took the light and peered into the sarcophagus.

'Well?' asked Ganniford growing impatient by his friend's silence.

'This man was known to me as Professor Harding. This is all most strange. Miss Eames, I wonder whether you would oblige us.'

'Good God, man, you can't expect a lady to look down at a corpse inside that thing!' protested Anstruther.

'If it would help us, Major, I am quite prepared to do so,' replied Miss Eames moving forward cautiously.

'Let me give you the lantern, my good lady,' said Jenkins.

Miss Eames took hold of the light and stared briefly into the tomb, before recoiling backwards.

'My dear lady, let me take your arm,' said Anstruther, placing a protective hand on the lady's shoulder.

'Would you care to take a seat, Miss Eames?' asked an anxious Hollinger.

'No, it is quite all right, gentlemen. I shall be well in a moment.'

'Did you recognize the man?' asked Ganniford eagerly.

'Yes. The gentleman was known to me only as a Mr Robarts.'

'This is, as you say in English, a most extraordinary state of affairs! It would appear that the deceased gentleman is known to all of us. In fact, I think it would be safe to conclude that it was this gentleman who was instrumental in our all being here tonight — and yet it would also appear that the said gentleman was known to each of us individually by a different name,' said Hollinger looking perplexed and rubbing his forehead with his hand.

'Good lord, Jenkins, this is a deuce fine mystery and no mistake!' exclaimed Ganniford.

'It looks as though our host did keep his appointment after all,' replied Jenkins.

'Mystery or not, what are we to do with the fellow?' asked Anstruther.

'What do you mean, Major — what are we to do with him?' enquired Hollinger.

'Well, undoubtedly he's dead, although he can't have been in there for long. Why don't we just push the lid back into its rightful position, and leave him inside?'

'We cannot do that, Major. It is only right and proper that we report this death to the proper authorities,' urged Hollinger.

'I agree with the major,' interrupted Ganniford. 'But if we do report this matter to the authorities, how the deuce are we going to explain our presence here tonight? It would look rather odd to say the least.'

'I am inclined to agree with you, Dr Hollinger. It is obvious that a crime has been committed, and as such we have a duty to report the matter,' said Jenkins.

'Miss Eames, what do you think?' asked Ganniford.

'I don't know what to think, gentlemen,' replied the lady shaking her head as she turned away from the scene.

'Look here, Hollinger, how do you think all this is going to look? Six people walking around the abbey at this time of night. There's bound to be some difficult questions to answer,' said Anstruther pacing up and down.

'The major is correct. It would look decidedly bad for us if we were to tell the authorities the real reason as to why we are all here tonight, trying to find the tomb of some medieval knight at such a late hour,' continued Ganniford.

'I must confess, my friend, that you may well have a point,' acknowledged Jenkins.

'Then let us put the top back on the tomb and leave as quickly as possible. No one would ever know that we have been here tonight,' urged Anstruther.

'I shouldn't do that, sir, if I were you!' said a gruff voice suddenly from out of the darkness.

The five members turned round quickly to see who had disturbed their conversation, and were alarmed to see a uniformed police officer standing before them holding a small lantern.

'Now then, gentlemen — and miss — would someone care to tell me what has been going on here tonight?'

CHAPTER ONE

LEDBURY, MARCH 1889

'Samuel.'

'Yes, my dear?' replied a voice from behind the newspaper.

'Are you familiar with the works of Mr Gilbert and Mr Sullivan?'

'When constabulary duty's to be done, to be done, the policeman's lot is not a happy one!' *came back the tuneful reply.*

'Samuel, I did not know that you had such a fine voice!'

'*Pirates of Penzance* — or is it *Pinafore*?' mused Ravenscroft, as he lowered his morning paper and stared at his wife through his spectacles, unsure as to whether she had just paid him a compliment, or had been merely teasing him over the breakfast table.

'Oh, I think it was the former,' replied Lucy. 'More tea?'

'Yes I believe it was the *Pirates* — although it could have been *Ruddigore*, the more I think about it,' said Ravenscroft resuming his reading.

'No, it was definitely *The Pirates of Penzance*.'

'If you say so. Why do you ask?'

'I read in the newspaper yesterday that Mr Gilbert and Mr Sullivan have composed a new operetta.' 'Really.'

'They call it *The Gondoliers*,' said Lucy, replenishing her husband's empty cup.

'Really,' said a uninterested voice from behind the paper.

'The critic in yesterday's newspaper has declared it to be one of their finest works.'

'Right.'

'The songs are said to be very witty.'

'Yes.'

'The sets are quite colourful, I believe,' persisted Lucy.

'Yes.'

'And the costumes are said to be quite striking in their design.'

'Really.'

'I wonder whether Mr Grossmith will be taking a role.'

'Perhaps.'

'Samuel, you could at least listen to what I am saying,' said a frustrated Lucy.

Ravenscroft lowered his newspaper once more. 'I am sorry, my dear, you were saying?'

'I was telling you about *The Gondoliers*, the new operetta by Mr Gilbert and Mr Sullivan.'

'Ah yes — and no doubt this work is being performed in London this very day.'

'The paper said the piece had been so well received, there was no reason that it should not run until the middle of the summer, at the very least. The critic in the *Illustrated London News* declared that it had been the finest thing he had seen this year. I was wondering whether we might undertake a short visit to — but no, you are far too busy,' said Lucy, turning away and looking out of the window.

'So this is what all this has been all about. You would like us to visit the capital to attend a performance of this *Gondoliers*,' said Ravenscroft smiling.

'Oh, Samuel, could we? I should so like to visit London. I have never been there, and have always wanted to go. We could go to one of the museums as well, or perhaps even Westminster Abbey. We need only be away for one night, if we caught the morning train?' said Lucy, excitedly, placing a hand on her husband's arm.

'And when were you thinking that we might undertake this excursion, my dear?' asked Ravenscroft.

'Well, we could go next week — or even this week. You do not seem to be particularly busy at the moment, and I am sure you must be eligible for a few days' relief. Oh do say yes, Samuel! I'm sure you would enjoy returning to London, even if only for a day or two, and I know you would so like to show me all your old familiar places,' continued Lucy, looking deeply into her husband's eyes.

'How can I, let alone any man, resist that beautiful, enticing smile of yours? Of course we shall go to London — and yes, you will see *The Gondoliers*.'

'Oh, Samuel, you are the most wonderful man in the world!' cried Lucy leaning across the table and planting a kiss on her husband's cheek.

'Excuse me, miss — sorry, Mrs Ravenscroft, Constable Crabb has just arrived and requests that he speaks with the master on urgent business,' interrupted the maid at the doorway.

'I'm sorry, my dear—' began Ravenscroft.

'Will you show Constable Crabb in, Susan?' said Lucy, leaning back in her chair and giving a slight sigh as she did so.

'Constable Crabb, sir,' announced the maid.

'Ah, Tom, do take a seat,' indicated Ravenscroft as the young, red-faced constable entered the room.

'Thank you, sir. Good morning to you, Mrs Ravenscroft,' replied Crabb accepting the seat.

'How are you, Tom?'

'Never better, ma'am.'

'And how is your wife Jennie and your adorable son?' enquired Lucy.

'Both very well, thank you, Mrs Ravenscroft.'

'Perhaps you would care to join us for breakfast?'

'No, thank you, ma'am, Jennie cooked me a fine repast before I left.'

'What can we do for you then, Tom?' asked Ravenscroft. 'You look a little out of breath.'

'I am sorry to intrude on your breakfast, sir, and Mrs Ravenscroft. I came as quickly as I could. The truth of the matter is, sir, that there appears to have been a terrible murder at Tewkesbury,' began the constable.

'Go on,' instructed Ravenscroft, laying his newspaper to one side and leaning forward.

'Apparently, last night, just after twelve, Constable Reynolds, the local town policeman, was going about his rounds when he happened to see a light flickering from inside the abbey. Upon further investigation he saw that the door to the building had been left slightly ajar and, as he slipped into the abbey, he could make out some voices inside. As he drew nearer, he saw what looked like a group of people all gathered round one of the tombs and upon closer investigation he found that the lid of the tomb had been forced open.'

'Interesting, tell me more,' said Ravenscroft, his curiosity aroused.

'Well, sir, it appears that there was a body inside the tomb.'

'I thought that's where they usually buried people, inside tombs' said Lucy.

'Ah yes, Mrs Ravenscroft, but this wasn't your usual collection of old bones, or decaying flesh, it was a freshly laid-out corpse, probably been killed that same day.'

'And someone, probably the killer, had deposited the body inside the tomb, with the object of concealment. How very strange. Do we know how this person died?' asked Ravenscroft.

'He had suffered a nasty blow to the back of his head.'

'You mentioned that Constable Reynolds had entered the abbey because he had first seen a light, and that there was a group of people standing around the tomb.'

'Yes, sir. There were five of them, four gents and a lady.'

'Did they offer any explanation as to their presence in the abbey at such a late hour?'

'Said they had been talking together at the Hop Pole and that one of them had suggested that they should go and visit the abbey to see the tombs.'

'But it was after twelve o'clock at night,' interjected Lucy.

'Exactly, ma'am.'

'This is all very interesting, Tom, but why are you telling me all this? Tewkesbury is out of my jurisdiction. Sergeant Braithwaite is in charge there, I believe — and how did you learn about this strange state of affairs?'

'That is correct, sir, but Sergeant Braithwaite has been ill of late, and is undertaking a few days' rest in Eastbourne.'

'Rather a long way to go,' remarked Ravenscroft.

'He has got relations there, so I understand.'

'I see.'

'Constable Reynolds made his way straight over to my house this morning, where he imparted all that had taken place. When I arrived at the station this morning I found this telegram had arrived there from headquarters, says you are to take charge of the case until Braithwaite returns,' said Crabb, reaching into his pocket and removing a piece of paper which he passed over to his superior.

'You are right, Crabb. "Proceed with all haste to Tewkesbury. Investigate murder in abbey",' read Ravenscroft.

'I've harnessed the trap, sir.'

'Then we should leave now, without delay. Excuse me, my dear,' said Ravenscroft rising from his chair.

'Of course,' said Lucy.

'I'm afraid *The Gondoliers* will have to wait for the present.'

'We can go later in the season,' said a resigned Lucy.

'When we shall certainly take in the museums, and the abbey as well. I think you will also enjoy St Paul's. Lead on, Tom.'

* * *

Later that morning as their trap approached the bridge that would take them into the town of Tewkesbury, Ravenscroft looked across the road to where old warehouses and tiny cottages fought for space along the banks of the river.

'I take it you have not visited Tewkesbury before today, sir?' asked Crabb.

'You are correct in your assumption, Tom.'

'It's a busy market-town, also popular with visitors at weekends who like to take trips along the river.'

Ravenscroft nodded as the trap approached an old inn with decorative flower baskets and rustic seats around its exterior. Crabb swung the vehicle sharply to their right and the pair found themselves travelling along the main street of the town, where a fine collection of four-storey, timber-framed buildings looked down upon their progress.

At the end of the road Crabb again turned the trap to their right, narrowly missing two young girls wearing pinafores and large hats who had been attempting to steer a pram from one side of the road to the other. Here, the Victoria Coffee Tavern looked across towards the Berkeley Arms Inn, the shop-front awnings and tall buildings cast long shadows on the ground and a number of half-laden carts stood idly by. A large building on their right announced itself to be the Hop Pole Hotel, its fine entrance portico attempting to enhance its importance.

'That's the abbey,' said Crabb pointing to his left.

'Rather a fine building,' said Ravenscroft alighting from the trap and beginning to make his way up the path that led to the main entrance. 'If I am not mistaken, I see someone is expecting us.'

'That will be Reynolds, sir. I told him to meet us here.'

'Good morning, sir,' said the stout, uniformed constable raising his hand to his temple.

'Reynolds,' acknowledged Ravenscroft.

'I took the liberty of forbidding all access to the abbey for the public, until after you had visited the scene of the crime, sir.'

'Good thinking, Reynolds. I trust the body has been removed to the mortuary?' asked Ravenscroft.

'It has, sir.'

'Constable Crabb has informed me of the circumstances of yesterday evening. You say it was the light from a lantern that first drew your attention to the building?'

'Yes, sir. Usually when I go past the abbey at that time of night, there is not a light to be seen inside and the main door is locked.'

'And when you entered the abbey you found a group of people standing round the open tomb.'

'That is correct, sir.'

'You questioned these people — there were five of them, I understand?'

'Yes, sir, four gentlemen and a lady.'

'And what explanation did they offer for their presence in the abbey at such a late hour?'

'Said they had been talking together at the Hop Pole over dinner, and that one of them had suggested that they should go and view the inside of the abbey.'

'And where are these people now?'

'They are at the Hop Pole, sir, just over the road. One of the gentlemen, of military bearing, said he was anxious to return to London. Said he had an urgent appointment to keep — but I told them that you would want to speak to them all upon your arrival here, sir, and that no one should leave the town before then.'

'Well done, Reynolds. You have acted well.'

'Thank you, sir,' replied the officer looking somewhat embarrassed by the compliment.

'Well, Crabb, we'd better go inside and see what all this is about,' said Ravenscroft.

'Oh, one word before you goes inside, sir.'

'Yes Constable?'

'Thought I ought to warn you, there's a religious gentleman, the Revd Jesterson — well, to put it mildly, he's in a bit of a state.'

'Obviously upset by last night's events,' suggested Ravenscroft.

'You are probably correct, sir. If you would care to follow me,' said the constable opening the door to the abbey.

The three men entered the building and, as they made their way down the nave of the church, they were met by a tall, thin gentleman dressed in a long clerical robe.

'Thank goodness you have come. What a terrible thing to have happened. Such violation, such desecration of God's house. What unholy person could have committed such an outrage?'

'Inspector Ravenscroft at your service, sir,' interjected Ravenscroft, breaking into the clergyman's agitated flow of words. 'And this is my associate, Constable Crabb. I believe you know Constable Reynolds already.'

'The Reverend Thomas Jesterson,' he replied, shaking Ravenscroft's hand. 'I am so relieved that you have arrived. This terrible occurrence is beyond all comprehension!'

'You are in charge of the abbey, sir?' asked Ravenscroft, hoping to calm the other's distressful outpourings by his line of questioning.

'I see to the day-to-day running of the building, but I—'

'Tell me, Reverend, is the building usually locked at night?' asked Ravenscroft.

'Why, yes, Inspector.'

'And was it locked last night?'

'Yes, I locked the building myself, at around eight o'clock.'

'Did you notice anything unusual at the time?'

'Unusual?'

'Yes. Did anything seem out of place? Did you notice any strangers wandering round the building?'

'No. There was no one here when I locked up the building. It was such an unpleasant evening, heavy rain and strong winds. I was quite anxious to return to my own home as quickly as possible.'

'But you definitely remember locking the abbey before you left.'

'I have just said that,' replied the clergyman.

'Does anyone else have access to the abbey, other than yourself?' asked Ravenscroft, observing that his previous question had caused the other some annoyance.

'The verger has the only other key.'

'And he is?'

'Trent. He resides at number five along the row of black and white buildings just to the side of the entrance to the abbey.'

'We will question him later. Perhaps you would be kind enough to show us the tomb where the stranger's body was found?'

'Yes, of course, I do hope you will be able to apprehend the perpetrators of this unseemly act,' said the reverend mopping his brow with a large handkerchief before leading the way further into the interior of the church.

'That is our intention, Reverend,' said Ravenscroft, trying to sound reassuring.

'Here we are, Inspector. Everything is as your constable found it yesterday evening,' said the clergyman stopping by a large monument at one side of the building.

'I see,' said Ravenscroft, placing one of his hands on the stone slab that formed the top of the tomb. 'It must have taken some effort to have raised this stone and to have lifted it across. I wonder how they managed to lift it. Ah, see here, Crabb, do you observe those marks on the side of the tomb? That must be where someone drove a wedge between the top slab and the rest of the monument. Then, when the wedge had been driven in, the top was moved to one side, just a few inches so that the person who committed this deed could look into the interior.'

'And just wide enough sir, for a body to be slid into the tomb,' added Crabb.

The two policemen looked at one another in bewilderment for some seconds.

'Excuse me, sir, but why did they go to all that trouble, when the body could have just been left on the floor?' asked Reynolds drawing nearer.

'Perhaps the killer was hoping to hide the body in the tomb, and then replace the top, so that no one would ever have found the dead man,' suggested Crabb.

'But if that was the case, why did he then leave it open? Reynolds, will you oblige us and try and see if you can replace the top of this tomb in its original position?' instructed Ravenscroft.

'Right, sir.'

Ravenscroft and Crabb stood back as Reynolds placed both his hands on the edge of the top stone and attempted to push it forward. 'I'm sorry, sir, I can't shift the thing!' he exclaimed, growing increasingly red in the face.

'Thank you, Reynolds. A valiant effort; you can ease off now. It is just as I thought. One man is not strong enough to move this stone on his own, whereas two might be more successful in the attempt.'

'You mean there were two despoilers of God's house?' exclaimed Jesterson.

'It would certainly have taken two men to have moved this stone, once the wedge had been driven into the gap. Let's have a look inside,' said Ravenscroft peering down into the interior of the monument.

'What can you see, sir?' asked Crabb.

'It is quite a way down to the bottom, almost six feet in depth I would say. There just seems to be a collection of old bones lying on the bottom.'

'Those "old bones", Inspector, as you put it so eloquently, are the mortal, sacred remains of Sir Roger de la Pole,' reprimanded Jesterson.

'I am sorry, I did not mean to cause any offence. What can you tell me about Sir Roger?' asked Ravenscroft quickly, as Crabb stepped up to gaze into the tomb.

'Sir Roger de la Pole was one of the Knights Templar who accompanied King Richard I on his Crusade to the Holy Land. He was a local benefactor and owned lands in the nearby villages of Deerhurst and Uckinghall, as well as here in Tewkesbury. He died shortly after his return from one of the crusades, and in his will left money to the abbey for prayers to be said, in perpetuity, for his soul and for the building of this monument to his memory,' replied the clergyman, warming to his subject.

'Smells a bit fusty inside,' remarked Crabb turning up his nose.

'You say that Sir Roger was a Knight Templar. Can you elaborate further, Reverend?' asked Ravenscroft, ignoring Crabb's comment.

'The Templars are an ancient order of knights originally formed in Jerusalem to protect pilgrims as they travelled to the holy land. They played an important role in the crusades in the twelfth and thirteenth centuries.'

'And what happened to them?'

'Unfortunately the brotherhood was suppressed in the early fourteenth century on the orders of the Pope and the King of France.'

'Why was that, sir?' interjected Crabb.

'It seems that the Templars had become very wealthy — they often acted as moneylenders — and that their prosperity caused a great deal of resentment.'

'What happened to them?' asked Ravenscroft.

'Many of them were put to death; a few escaped and travelled to places like Rhodes and Malta, which they defended against the forces of the Infidel.'

'You seem very well informed, Reverend,' said Ravenscroft.

'The abbey attracts a great many visitors, particularly in the summer months, and many of them often enquire about the origins of the tomb.'

'I have seen a number of tombs of this period and many of them have carved effigies either on the top or at the sides,' said Ravenscroft.

'You are correct, Mr Ravenscroft, but in this case the tomb is quite plain.'

'Is that unusual?'

'It is not uncommon.'

'How do we know then that this the tomb of Sir Roger?' asked Crabb.

'If you look down towards the bottom of the tomb, just here on the side, you will see that the name of Sir Roger de la Pole has been carved into the stone.'

Ravenscroft and Crabb knelt down and examined the engraved lettering. 'I see, yes, here is the name of Sir Roger. What are these numbers and letters below the name?' asked Ravenscroft staring at the carving and running his fingers over the stone.

'I'm afraid I cannot help you there, Inspector. We often get enquiries about the inscription, but we are at a loss as to their true meaning. They don't appear to relate to dates of birth or death of Sir Roger, and we have even tried to replace the numbers and letters with various known ciphers, but without success.'

'Very interesting,' said Ravenscroft standing upright. 'Crabb, make a note of the inscription in your pocket book.'

'Yes, sir,' replied the constable copying down the letters and numbers:

CR4 * Q1 * BR3 * CR4 * Q1 * Q2
BL2 * KL2 * +3 * CL2 * Q2 * CR1 * CL1

'Thank you, Reverend, you have been most helpful and informative. Be assured that my colleague and myself will do all that we can to fully investigate this matter and bring the perpetrators of this deed to book.'

'Before you leave, Inspector, I wonder if we could replace the slab on top of the tomb? It is only right and proper that Sir Roger should be allowed to rest in peace, away from prying eyes.'

'Of course. Reynolds, Crabb, help me to push the stone back into its rightful place.'

* * *

'Did the body have any means of identification upon him?' enquired Ravenscroft.

'None whatsoever I'm afraid, Inspector.'

Ravenscroft and Crabb had left the abbey a few minutes previously and were now standing in the cold, damp, mortuary building and staring down at the naked corpse which lay before them on an old wooden table. Two candles flickered uneasily in the darkened room and an old iron tap dripped loudly into a cracked stone sink in the corner.

'There were no letters about his person or any other documents?'

'His pockets were completely empty,' replied the doctor, wiping his bloodstained hands on a towel.

'Obviously his killer did not want anyone to be able to identify his victim. What can you tell us about his injuries?'

'The poor man suffered a large blow on the back of his head; that is what killed him.'

'What kind of instrument do you think was used to kill him, Doctor?' continued Ravenscroft.

'I would think by the size of the blow that it must have been a very heavy object of some kind.'

'A hammer, or mallet, perhaps?'

'It could well have been.'

'What do we make of this fellow then, Crabb?' asked Ravenscroft, bending over the body.

'I would say he was about forty years of age, sir, slightly smaller in height than the average, with no signs of starvation, nor any other injuries,' said Crabb, after a few moments of deliberation.

'Good. Go on.'

'I don't think he was used to any kind of hard labour.'

'Why do you say that, Crabb?'

'His hands and feet look too soft.'

'Well done, but I think we can go further and conclude that he was probably a clerk by profession, and that he was also left-handed.'

'How do you know that, sir?' asked a puzzled Crabb.

'Look at his hands and you will observe the ink stains on his thumb and next two fingers of his left hand, whereas there are none on his right hand. I think that if we were to examine his clothes we might also well find signs of ink on the left cuff of his shirt.'

Crabb walked over to the chair, where the deceased's clothes had been placed and picked up the item in question. 'I do believe you're right, sir.'

'Although there are ink stains on the cuffs, there is not a great deal of wear on the garment, suggesting that it was either a recent purchase, or that its owner had taken particular care of it,' said Ravenscroft, joining his colleague and examining the shirt before turning towards the remainder of the dead man's clothes. 'In fact, the suit, although not expensive and of a plain, ordinary nature in its design, is of a smart, presentable appearance, suggesting that our friend liked to dress well. I would say that although he was a clerk by profession, he was nevertheless not of a lower station. This man either worked in a senior capacity in an office, or took steps to see that his appearance created an impression of far greater importance than his actual position in life. Unfortunately there are no labels in any of the garments to enable us to trace them back to their place of sale.'

'Looks as though our victim will go unnamed,' added Crabb.

'Let us take a look at the deceased's shoes.'

Crabb handed them to Ravenscroft, who examined them both inside and out.

'I would say these are what you would call, London shoes, being extremely well made and of a fairly expensive nature. Our unknown stranger seems to have spent more money on that item than the rest of his apparel, suggesting perhaps that a recent investment had borne fruit.'

'I will leave you two gentlemen to your deliberations,' said the doctor who had been standing quietly by during the conversation.

'Yes, thank you, Doctor,' said Ravenscroft, as the medical man left the room. 'Did you notice anything else unusual about the corpse, Crabb?'

'I don't believe so, sir.'

'Look again at his feet. The nails on his left foot have been recently clipped, whereas the nails on his right foot are quite long,' said Ravenscroft, returning to the table and bending over the deceased man.

'Now you mention it, sir, you are quite right. What an odd thing to do. Why cut the nails on one foot and not the other? What do you make of it?'

'I don't. I cannot see the significance at all.'

'What do we do now? Shall I circulate his description to the local newspaper and nearby police station? Someone might know who he is,' suggested Crabb making notes in his pocket book. 'He might have been staying locally, so it might be worth our while making enquiries at the local hostelries.'

'By all means, Tom, but it may be of little avail if he had just recently arrived in the town. Let us gather together what we know about our friend. We have a middle-aged clerk, of less than average stature, who cuts the nails on one of his feet but not the other, and who dresses well, but not extravagantly so, except for his shoes, and who probably originates from London. Now we have to ask ourselves — what was such a gentleman as this doing in the abbey in Tewkesbury late yesterday evening — and why was he killed in such a brutal fashion and then placed in a tomb belonging to a medieval knight?'

'I must admit, sir, that I am at a complete loss,' said Crabb replacing his notebook in the top pocket of his tunic.

'When we were in the abbey just now, we wondered why the top stone had not been replaced on the monument. I think that this man and one other broke into the abbey yesterday evening between the hours of eight and twelve, where they drove a wedge under the lid of the tomb, until they were able to lift it up enough to be able to move it slightly to one side so that they could look down into its interior,' said Ravenscroft, removing his spectacles and cleaning the lenses on his handkerchief.

'Whatever for, sir?' asked Crabb. 'There's only a load of old bones inside — old Sir Roger. Who would want those?'

'There may be just old Sir Roger's bones there now, but what if there was something else inside the tomb? Yes of course! There must have been something else lying next to the bones on the floor of the tomb. You noticed how tall the monument was. If there was something lying there, it would have been impossible to have reached over and secured the item,' said Ravenscroft, replacing his spectacles and becoming increasingly animated.

'You mean our man climbed into the tomb—'

'—To secure whatever lay there, and after he had passed the item on to his companion, that was when the second man hit him on the head!'

'That's why the killer could not replace the top stone!'

'Exactly, Crabb. He could not move the stone on his own, and so he left it as we found it.'

'I wonder what was taken from the inside of the tomb?'

'That is what we have to find out. No doubt once we have found what was taken, then we will be able to arrest our killer. I wonder why the deceased man and his companion come to Tewkesbury — and what was in the tomb that was so important to them? And what were those five people doing gathered round the tomb at such a late hour? What had brought them all to the abbey on such an inhospitable night? I tell you something, Crabb, this has all the makings of a strange and baffling case, and no mistake, the sooner we commence our investigations the better we will be placed to arrive at a solution.'

CHAPTER TWO

TEWKESBURY

'Intolerable! This is just intolerable!'

Ravenscroft looked up from his desk in the snug of the Hop Pole at the irate military gentleman who had just strode into the room. 'Major Anstruther, I believe. Would you care to take a seat?'

'Your constable has prevented me from leaving; I tell you this delay is not to be borne, sir!

'This is a very serious matter, sir—'

'I don't care how serious this is; the fact remains that I am expected to rejoin my regiment later today in London.'

'And what regiment would that be, sir?' asked Ravenscroft, looking down at the papers before him and trying to sound as calm as possible.

'The Guards, man! The Guards!' exclaimed Anstruther, staring intently at the balding, middle-aged man and the young, fresh-faced constable.

'Of course, I should have known. If you would be kind enough to answer a few questions for us, we will try not to detain you too long. Please take a seat, Major.'

'Intolerable! I don't see what all this has to do with me anyway,' replied Anstruther reluctantly accepting the chair.

'You were in the abbey yesterday evening, when the body was discovered. You don't deny that?'

'Of course I was in the abbey, man!' retorted Anstruther.

'Then perhaps you would care to tell Constable Crabb and myself what you were doing inside the building at such a late hour, standing next to an opened tomb which contained the remains of an unknown person who had been brutally murdered that same evening?' enquired Ravenscroft leaning back in his chair and looking directly at his suspect.

'I know it looks bad, Inspector, but there is a simple explanation for all this, I can assure you.'

'Please proceed, Major Anstruther.'

'We had all been conversing together with one another, in this very room, earlier in the evening—'

'You say "we" — could you elaborate further?'

'Yes; Ganniford, Jenkins, Miss Eames, Dr Hollinger. We had all arrived in the town earlier that day, and were enjoying a pleasant evening together when someone suggested that we should all go and take a tour round the abbey, take in the monuments and such like.'

'At twelve o'clock at night?' asked Ravenscroft.

'I know it sounds rather strange, but we had all been drinking a lot and thought it would be rather interesting to go and see the relics.'

'And what happened next?'

'We all went across to the abbey, went inside the building and started to look round at the monuments. Then someone noticed that the lid of one of the tombs had been moved. We naturally looked inside and found the remains of that poor fellow. Then one of your constables came up to us — and the rest you know.'

'Did you know who the deceased gentleman was?'

'No, never seen him before,' replied Anstruther stroking his moustache and looking down at the floor.

'You are sure on that point?'

'I've just said, I had never seen the person before,' snapped the major, glaring at his questioner.

'Tell me, Major, what were you doing in Tewkesbury?'

'I don't see that is any of your business.'

'I'm afraid, sir, everything is my business when murder is concerned. What were you doing in the town?' repeated Ravenscroft firmly.

'Nothing of any importance.'

'That is for me to decide.'

'Damn it, man, if you must know I had been visiting a lady in Bristol, was on the way back to London to rejoin my regiment and decided to put up in the town for the night.'

'Could we have the name of this lady?'

'No, you certainly may not. Question of honour and all that. Can't do.'

'I see. Tell me, had any of your companions been previously known to you before yesterday evening; had you met any of them before?' asked Ravenscroft realizing that he would have to change his line of questioning.

'No, never seen any of them before. We just met up here, had dinner and a drink together and fell into conversation.'

'Can you tell me whose idea it was to go and explore the abbey at such a late hour?'

'Er, I don't think I can remember. I believe it just came up in the general conversation.'

'Try and remember, Major. It is most important. Whose idea was it to visit the abbey?' repeated Ravenscroft leaning forward.

'Well I suppose it might have been that Prussian doctor, Hollinger. Yes, I think he suggested the visit.'

'Thank you, Major. I think that will be all for now.'

'I presume that I can now return to London?' asked Anstruther, rising from his chair.

'I'm afraid not.'

'Oh, come on, man. I've told you everything I can. I don't see how I can be of any further use to you.'

'I'm sorry, sir, but murder is a very serious matter and we may well need to speak to you again. It would be appreciated if you would kindly rejoin the others in the other room and wait there until I have questioned your companions.'

'Waste of time, man. They will only tell you what I have said. Can't expect anything different. Look, what am I to tell my regiment?'

'May I suggest you send them a telegram explaining that your return will be delayed?' suggested Ravenscroft.

'Damn all this, Ravenscroft! All this is an infernal inconvenience!' said Anstruther, banging his fist down suddenly on the table.

'As soon as I have questioned your companions and discovered who killed the man in the tomb, then you will be free to leave and rejoin your regiment,' replied Ravenscroft, ignoring the outburst and looking down at the papers before him.

'Damned inconvenience!' exclaimed Anstruther striding out of the room and banging the door behind him.

'Well, he certainly seems annoyed,' said Crabb looking up from his notebook from the corner of the room where he had been seated witnessing the interview.

'That's as may be.'

'Do you believe all that talk about a lady in Bristol, point of honour and all that?'

'Oh I'm sure he made all that up. But did you also notice, Tom, how he looked away quickly when I asked him if he had ever seen the deceased man before? I'm sure the two men had met. No, I think our major was not telling us the truth. I don't believe for one minute that he just happened to arrive here on his way back to London. He was here in Tewkesbury because he had arranged to meet someone.'

'The other members of the group?' suggested Crabb.

'Maybe,' replied Ravenscroft. 'Either way I don't think we are going to obtain more from Major Anstruther just now. I think we should next turn our attention to Dr Hollinger. Anstruther said he thought it was Hollinger who had put forward the idea of the nocturnal excursion. Be so good, Crabb, as to ask the learned doctor to join us.'

'As you wish, sir,' replied the constable leaving the room.

Ravenscroft rose from his seat and looked out of the window, to where the distant sound of people talking and carts travelling along the cobbled streets could be heard. Then his eyes looked across the road towards the great abbey which seemed to dominate all that was before it, as it had done so for many past centuries. He had the feeling that this was going to be a difficult case.

'Doctor Hollinger, sir,' said Crabb, disturbing his thoughts as he re-entered the room.

'Inspector Ravenscroft,' said the new arrival extending a hand.

'Doctor Hollinger. I am pleased to make your acquaintance, sir. Would you please take a seat?' replied Ravenscroft, shaking the doctor's hand.

'This is a terrible business, Inspector, terrible,' said Hollinger, shrugging his shoulders and accepting the chair.

'Quite so, sir. I hope you don't mind assisting us in our enquiries?'

'Of course not.'

'Thank you, sir. I wonder if we might begin with a few facts concerning yourself.'

'Certainly. I am of Prussian extraction. My name is Doctor Andreas Hollinger. I am a medical practitioner in Baden-Baden. Patients come there when they are sick to, er, how you say, to take the waters. You may know of such treatments.'

'I am very familiar with the water cure treatments,' replied Ravenscroft, giving a slight smile in his constable's direction. 'May I ask, Doctor, the purpose of your visit to Tewkesbury?'

'Certainly; I had been visiting a colleague of mine in Cheltenham for a few days. We had compared notes on the effectiveness of the water treatments. I was about to spend a day or two in London before returning home, and decided to stop off at Tewkesbury for the evening.'

'Could you give us the name of this doctor in Cheltenham?'

'Why? I do not see—'

'We just need to confirm your account, Doctor,' said Ravenscroft, observing the elderly doctor's unease.

'I still do not see why you need to know the name of my fellow practitioner.'

'If you could oblige us, sir,' persisted Ravenscroft.

'Er, let me see. It was Dr Meadows. Yes, Dr Meadows.'

'Thank you — and what transpired yesterday evening?'

'Pardon? Transpired?' asked Hollinger looking perplexed.

'What took place yesterday evening?'

'Ah yes, you say transpired. I fell in conversation with a group of my fellow guests, and then we went over to the abbey where we found that unfortunate man.'

'Had you met any members of the group before yesterday evening?'

'No. They were all new to me.'

'And the man inside the tomb, had you ever met him before?'

'No.'

'You said just now that you fell into conversation with your fellow guests. What sort of things did you talk about?'

'I am sorry, I do not understand.'

'I would just to like to know what you and your fellow guests talked about yesterday evening.'

'Well, I cannot remember everything, Inspector, but I will try.'

'If you would be so kind.'

'Let me see — the weather; you English always talk about the weather. Wherever I go there is always the weather to talk about,' smiled Hollinger. 'It was very bad last night. Rain "cats and um dogs", as you say.'

'Anything else?'

'We talked about the town, how pleasant it appeared, and yes, the hotel.'

'Whose idea was it to go and visit the abbey at such a late hour?' asked Ravenscroft, looking directly at the practitioner.

'Visit the abbey?' repeated Hollinger rubbing his forehead.

'Yes, Doctor, who suggested that you should visit the abbey?'

'I cannot be sure.'

'Try and remember, Doctor,' urged Ravenscroft.

'Ah yes, it was Herr Jenkins. Yes, Mr Jenkins who proposed that we should visit the abbey. I believe that to be the case.'

'Would it not have been better to have waited until the morning, sir?' asked Crabb.

'I suppose you are correct, Constable, it would have been better to have gone in the morning, but one or two people said that they had to leave very early, and we all thought it would be an excellent opportunity to go then.'

'But surely the abbey would have been locked up at that hour of the night?' suggested Ravenscroft.

'I do not know. In Baden we do not lock up our religious buildings for the evening. They are open all the time.'

'And how did you find the abbey when you arrived?'

'Sorry, "find the abbey". I do not understand.'

'Did you find the abbey open or closed? Did someone have a key?'

'Ah yes, I understand. The abbey was not locked.'

'I see. Thank you, Doctor, for answering all my questions.'

'I am glad that I was of assistance, Inspector. May I go now?'

'I would be obliged if you would wait with the others. I'm afraid I cannot allow any of you to leave the town until after we have completed our inquiries.'

'I quite understand,' said Hollinger rising from his seat, as Crabb walked over to open the door.

'Oh one last question, Dr Hollinger — when you were in the abbey, who first noticed the opened tomb?' asked Ravenscroft.

'I believe it was myself, Inspector.'

'And how did you know the tomb belonged to the Templar Knight?'

'I did not, until I leaned down and saw the name on the side.'

Ravenscroft nodded as Hollinger left the room. 'Close the door, Crabb. Well, what do you make of our foreign gentleman?'

'I think he knows more than he wanted to tell us,' replied Crabb.

'My thoughts exactly. He was not very forthcoming with the name of his fellow doctor in Cheltenham. We will need to confirm his story. Doctor Meadows I think he said. Also I do not quite believe that he would have stopped the night in Tewkesbury on the way back to London, when he could have taken a more direct route from Cheltenham. Tewkesbury would have been out of his way.'

'Perhaps he wanted to see the abbey and the town before his return to London,' suggested Crabb.

'Maybe. Then he seemed to have some difficulty in recalling the details of last night's conversation, and what was actually said. When I pressed him all he could think about was that they discussed the weather.'

'He also said that it was Jenkins who proposed the visit to the abbey, whereas Anstruther claimed that it was Hollinger who came up with the idea.'

'Yes, you picked that up as well. So we now have two different accounts as to whose idea it was to visit the abbey. I have the distinct impression that we are not being told the truth.'

'Shall I ask Jenkins to come in next?'

'No, I think we will leave Ganniford and Jenkins until later. Let us see whether Miss Eames can enlighten us further.'

Crabb left the room and returned a few moments later with his charge.

'My dear Miss Eames,' said Ravenscroft rising from his chair. 'I am sorry that you have been caught up in this affair. I appreciate you must find all this rather distressing, but I am afraid I must ask you a few questions if you don't mind.'

'I quite understand,' replied the lady, accepting the seat which Crabb had indicated.

'Thank you, Miss Eames. I wonder whether we might begin with the reason for your visit to Tewkesbury.'

'The reason for my visit?'

'If you would be so kind,' smiled Ravenscroft.

'For the past few years I have nursed my father, who has been very ill. We live in Ludlow in Shropshire. Recently my father passed away and I found myself quite alone in the world,' replied the lady, in a quietly spoken unassuming manner.

'I am sorry for your loss, Miss Eames,' interrupted Ravenscroft, observing the other's composure.

'I, er . . . I decided that I would like to travel for a while, something which I had not been able to do during my father's long illness. I had always wished to see Bath. I thought that Tewkesbury would be a pleasant place to call upon during my travels.'

'So you arrived here yesterday?'

'In the early afternoon.'

'And what happened in the evening?'

'We went across to the abbey.'

'No, before that.'

'Oh, I see. During dinner my fellow travellers and myself were discussing the antiquities of the town and someone suggested that we should go and visit the abbey.'

'Can you remember who proposed the idea?' asked Ravenscroft.

'I don't really recall. Is it important?'

'It would help us a great deal in our investigations if you could try and remember, Miss Eames,' smiled Ravenscroft.

'Oh yes, I think it was Major Anstruther.'

Ravenscroft looked across at Crabb. 'Major Anstruther you say. You are sure on that point?'

'I think so, or was it Mr Ganniford? No, I do believe it was the major.'

'It was rather late to venture out to the abbey, and on such an inclement night as well. Would it not perhaps have been more suitable to have delayed your visit until the morning?'

'Yes, you are quite right, inspector. It was all rather foolish of us I suppose, particularly in the light of what happened. I did not really want to accompany the others, but I felt that now that the visit had been suggested and everyone was quite anxious to go, it would seem churlish of me not to have gone with them,' replied the lady looking distractedly at the floor.

'I quite understand. So you all walked over to the abbey together?'

'Yes.'

'And what happened when you arrived there?'

'We walked around the abbey, together, all six of us — sorry, five of us.'

'It must have been very dark?' offered Crabb.

'We took two lanterns with us.'

'Please continue, Miss Eames,' encouraged Ravenscroft.

'Well, we just walked, examining the various monuments, until we came to that dreadful open tomb with that poor man inside,' replied the lady suddenly faltering in her speech and drawing a handkerchief to her eyes.

'I'm sorry, Miss Eames. Perhaps you would like some water?'

'Thank you,' she replied, taking the glass from Crabb and sipping the liquid.

'I appreciate this must have been all very upsetting for you,' said Ravenscroft, trying to sound as sympathetic as he could.

'I am so sorry. Please forgive me. I am not usually like this. It was just when I saw that man inside that tomb, I suddenly remembered the funeral of my poor late father—'

'My dear Miss Eames, please do not distress yourself,' said Ravenscroft rising from his seat and placing a hand upon her shoulder. 'Perhaps you would prefer another time to answer our questions?'

'Thank you. You are most kind. It might indeed be better. I'm so sorry. I am not usually like this,' replied the lady, dabbing her eyes.

'Crabb, would you please escort Miss Eames back to the other room. I am afraid I must ask you to stay with the others until we have completed our inquiries,' said Ravenscroft, opening the door.

'Of course, Inspector. I understand.'

After the others had left the room, Ravenscroft returned to his desk where he busied himself in polishing the lens of his spectacles.

'Well, she put on a fine act and no mistake,' said Crabb returning from the outer room.

'Tom, I do believe you are becoming rather cynical in your young age,' smiled Ravenscroft. 'I believe that she was genuinely distressed. I can appreciate that seeing that dead man lying in the open tomb must have been upsetting to her, coming shortly after the burial of her own father. Interesting though that she thought it was Jenkins who had suggested the visit to the abbey, when our two previous speakers claimed otherwise. The more I interview these people, the more I am coming to the conclusion that they are not telling us the truth.'

'Who would you like next, sir — Ganniford or Jenkins?'

'Oh, let us have the pair of them in together,' sighed Ravenscroft, 'After all, I believe they travelled here to Tewkesbury together, from what Reynolds was saying.'

Before Crabb could leave the room however, the door was abruptly thrown open and a large, red-faced man of more than ample girth strode up to Ravenscroft's desk. 'Look here, my man, we are confoundedly annoyed with having to loiter around all morning waiting to be seen!'

'I'm sorry to have kept you, gentlemen; we had to question your companions first, as I am sure you will appreciate,' said Ravenscroft, trying not be put off by this sudden intrusion.

'Blessed if I will appreciate it, sir!' retorted the new arrival, wheezing as he spoke.

'You must excuse my colleague's impetuosity,' said the second, grey-haired, thin-faced, gentleman entering the room.

'Perhaps you would both care to take a seat, gentlemen? I hope not to detain you for very much longer.'

'I sincerely hope not, sir,' grumbled the fat gentleman.

'I am sure the inspector will be as quick as he can with his questions, Ganniford,' said the elder gentleman accepting a seat and seeking to placate his companion.

'Thank you gentlemen. I understand that both of you are acquainted with one another?' asked Ravenscroft.

'Mr Ganniford and I have known one another for the past fifteen years,' replied Jenkins.

'I presume that you travelled to Tewkesbury together?'

'Of course we did,' grumbled Ganniford, sinking into the chair.

'Can I ask the reason for your visit to Tewkesbury?'

'We had reason to visit the Ashmolean in Oxford, and thought we might like to extend our stay by several days, exploring Tewkesbury and the surrounding area, before our return to London,' said Jenkins in a matter-of-fact voice.

'May I ask where you reside in London?' enquired Ravenscroft.

'Don't see what that has to do with this affair,' complained Ganniford.

'My colleague resides in Suffolk Gardens, I have rooms near Lincoln's Inn,' offered Jenkins.

'Why did you decide to visit the abbey yesterday evening?' asked Ravenscroft changing the subject of his questioning.

'We had been talking together over dinner. Miss Eames was saying that she had always wanted to visit the abbey to view the monuments there, so it was decided that we would go and have a tour round the place,' offered Ganniford.

'Who decided that, sir?'

'How the blazes do you expect us to remember that?' complained Ganniford. 'It cannot be of any great importance who suggested the visit.'

'I think it is of the greatest importance,' said Ravenscroft, leaning back in his chair and studying the two men.

'I believe it was probably the major,' said Jenkins.

'Thank you, sir. It was rather late in the evening to go visiting the abbey,' suggested Ravenscroft. 'And I believe it was raining quite heavily.'

'Not afraid of the weather; rain never hurt anyone,' mumbled Ganniford.

'I know, Mr Ravenscroft, that it must appear rather strange to you that a group of strangers should all decide to visit the abbey at such a late hour, but we had all been talking so earnestly together and none of us wished to wait until the morning to begin our journey of exploration,' said Jenkins, staring over the top of his glasses at Ravenscroft.

'Wanted to see the tomb of that Templar fellow,' added Ganniford.

'Ah yes, Sir Roger de la Pole. You must be acquainted with the life of the knight?' asked Ravenscroft, addressing Jenkins.

'I know that Sir Roger was one of the Knights Templar, that he made at least one journey to the Holy Land and that he finally settled and died in this area, hence the reason for his entombment in the abbey. That is all I am afraid I can tell you,' replied Jenkins.

'So you went in search of Sir Roger yesterday evening?'

'I would not say, Inspector, that we went to the abbey with the main intention of finding Sir Roger's tomb. There are plenty of other fine relics inside the building that we wished to see.'

'How did you know, Mr Jenkins, that the building would be open at such a late hour?'

'We did not. I suppose we all hoped that the abbey would be open.'

'And if it was not?'

'Then we would almost certainly have returned in the morning,' replied Jenkins, attempting a smile.

'When you reached the abbey, what did you do next?'

'Went inside,' grumbled Ganniford shrugging his broad shoulders.

'It must have been very dark?' suggested Crabb.

'We had two lanterns with us,' said Jenkins.

'And did you walk round the abbey together, or on your own?' continued Ravenscroft.

'Miss Eames, Mr Ganniford and myself took one lantern, the others the remaining lantern,' answered the older man.

'And who was it that discovered the opened tomb?'

'Doctor Hollinger. He called us over to the other side of the abbey, and that was when we found that unfortunate man.'

'Had you ever seen the dead man before?' asked Ravenscroft.

'Certainly not! Never clapped eyes on the fellow,' snapped Ganniford.

'And you, Mr Jenkins, had you ever met the deceased?'

'I believe not.'

'Did you hear or see anything else in the abbey — perhaps someone moving around, or leaving the building?'

'No. I don't recall seeing anything else. What about you, Ganniford, did you see anything?'

'Can't say I did,' replied his companion.

'Tell me, gentlemen, had you ever met Major Anstruther, Miss Eames or Dr Hollinger before yesterday evening?' asked Ravenscroft.

'No. Never seem 'em before in my life. What's all that got to do with that dead fellow?' asked Ganniford.

'I just wondered whether you were previously known to one another.'

'No, Inspector Ravenscroft, last night was the first time we had all met,' added Jenkins.

'Look here, Inspector, I'm sure we have told you everything we know. We realize that all this is an unfortunate affair, but Mr Jenkins and myself must really return to London on the afternoon train,' said Ganniford irritably.

'I'm afraid, gentlemen, that we have to fully investigate this "unfortunate affair" as you so described it, so I would be obliged if you would all remain here for a while longer,' said Ravenscroft.

'Oh, come, man, this is all so absurd—' protested Ganniford.

'We quite understand, Inspector,' interjected Jenkins, 'I'm sure we can wait a little longer, Ganniford. We have a duty to assist the inspector in his inquiries. After all a man has been killed. There is always the evening train.'

'Suppose so. Dashed inconvenient and all that,' sighed Ganniford, with an air of reluctance.

'Thank you, gentlemen.'

The two men left the room, the younger muttering under his breath, the elder placing a reassuring arm on his friend's shoulder.

'An odd couple,' said Crabb.

'I believe Mr Jenkins is what you might call, an antiquary. Ganniford can best be described as a gentleman of leisure. I believe that neither of them was telling us the truth. But then I do not think that the other members of the party were either. I do not believe that they all just fell into conversation last night, and then decided to visit the abbey, at such a late hour as well, and on such a bad evening, because one of them suddenly decided that it would be a good idea. Each one of them claims that it was a different person who came up with the idea. Hollinger and Miss Eames's account of the evening's conversation seem different from one another, and I am certain that more than one of them had met the deceased man before. The only thing they agree on is that it was Hollinger who found the opened tomb first.'

'What are we going to do next, sir?'

'I find it strange that the abbey was open at such a late hour. The Reverend Jesterson said that the building was locked when he left at eight, so why was it open at twelve that evening? I will go and see this fellow Trent, who is the verger. Apparently he has the other key. He may know something. Meanwhile I would like you, Tom, to pay a visit to the local library, and see if you can find out if these people are who they say they are,' said Ravenscroft rising from his seat.

'How will I do that, sir?' asked Crabb, licking the point of his pencil.

'Directories. The library should have a local Gloucestershire directory, so find out if this Dr Meadows is listed as practising in Cheltenham. They will probably have a London directory as well, so see if Jenkins and Ganniford are resident in the places they say. I doubt if you will find a directory for Shropshire, but if you are fortunate in that direction, you can look up the Eames family in Ludlow — and check the latest Army List for Anstruther.'

'Right, sir,' replied Crabb writing furiously in his notebook, 'And what about our friends in the other room?'

'I shall have to tell them that they are to remain here for a while longer, whilst we are continuing with our investigations.'

'That will go down well.'

'That's as may be. Perhaps a little enforced delay might encourage them to be more forthcoming with their answers.'

* * *

A few minutes later Ravenscroft stood outside one of the old cottages that ran in a row along the side of the street outside the abbey. The brass plate next to the knocker was engraved with the word 'Verger' in neat italic lettering.

'Good morning to you, sir. Am I correct in assuming that I am speaking with Mr Trent?' said Ravenscoft addressing the rather scruffily dressed, unshaven, bleary-eyed, grey-haired man who opened the door to him.

'That depends on who wants him. My head be all-about today.'

'My name is Ravenscroft. Inspector Ravenscroft of the local constabulary. I am carrying out an investigation into the body that was found in the abbey last night. I would like to ask you a few questions.'

'Nothin' to do with me,' replied the old man, rubbing his head and turning away from Ravenscroft. 'I knows nothin' about any dead body.'

'Your name is Trent?'

'I might be.'

'Are you Trent or not?' asked Ravenscroft, becoming annoyed.

'No need to caddle,' protested the man.

'I understand that you are responsible for locking up the cathedral each evening,' said Ravenscroft, ignoring the last comment.

'I locks building up if Reverend ain't there.'

'And did you lock up the building last night?'

'No. Reverend did that. We both left together.'

'What time was that?'

'Can't remember,' grumbled the verger, rubbing his head again.

'Try and remember. It is most important,' insisted Ravenscroft.

'Just after eight it were.'

'Did you go back to the abbey after that time?'

'No — why should I?'

'I ask because at twelve o'clock last night a group of visitors found the door open,' said Ravenscroft.

'Well, I didn't open it,' grumbled the verger.

'Then how do you account for it being open?'

'How should I know?' replied the other turning away and attempting to close the door.

'This is a very serious matter, Mr Trent. Sometime between eight and twelve yesterday evening two people were able to enter the abbey, and one of them was murdered there and placed inside one of the tombs,' said Ravenscroft, placing his hand on the door to prevent its closure.

'Perhaps it was that miserable fellow then.'

'What miserable fellow?'

'The one that banged on me door last night.'

'I'm sorry, I don't quite understand,' said Ravenscroft, hoping that this line of questioning might be leading somewhere.

'Came to my house and asked me to open up the abbey for him.'

'What time was this?'

'About nine. Said he would give me six shillings if I would meet him and his friends outside the abbey at twelve and let 'em all in.'

'I see — and did you go to the abbey at the appointed time?'

'More than my job's worth. Went to the Nailers instead.'

'The Nailers?'

'Jerry-house, up other end of town. You can ask 'em there if you likes. They will tell you I was there from eleven to nearly one.'

'So this man came to your house at around nine o'clock and asked you to meet him and his colleagues outside the abbey later that evening, but you went to the Nailers instead.'

'That's what I said. Wish I 'adn't gone. I be all a middling this morning.'

'Can you describe this man who wanted you to meet him outside the abbey?'

'Miserable he were.'

'Can you be a little more precise. Was he young, old, thin, fat?' asked Ravenscroft.

''Course I can. I ain't half-soaked. Thin-faced man he were, grey-haired getting on in years, wore spectacles on end of long, thin nose, spoke in a dull old voice. Will that be all?'

'Thank you, Mr Trent, you have been most helpful.'

The verger closed the door abruptly in Ravenscroft's face.

* * *

'Well, Tom, what did you manage to discover at the library?' asked Ravenscroft, as the two men met up later outside the Hop Pole.

'Library seems an untidy place. Books everywhere, and the librarian is a strange fellow. Can't understand what he was saying half the time. Found out some interesting things though, sir,' replied Crabb taking out his pocket-book.

'Go on,' urged Ravenscroft.

'I looked in the local directory. There was no entry for anyone called Dr Meadows in Cheltenham.'

'I thought so. So Hollinger was lying. Go on, Tom.'

'They did have a London directory, and Ganniford and Jenkins are both listed at the places they said — Suffolk Square and near Lincoln's Inn Fields. The library also had the Army List for the past three years but I could not find any record of a Major Anstruther being listed.'

'That's interesting. It would appear then that our major is not perhaps who he claims to be. And Miss Eames?'

'They didn't have a directory for Shropshire, sir.'

'No matter, we can always send a telegram later to the local station in Ludlow.'

'How did you get on with Trent, sir?' asked Crabb replacing his notebook in the upper pocket of his tunic.

'Trent remembers Jesterson locking up the building at eight. Apparently an hour later a gentleman visited his house and engaged Trent's services to open up the abbey for him at twelve that evening.'

'That would explain why the abbey was open.'

'Ah, but Trent never kept the appointment. He went drinking at one of the local inns instead.'

'So if this Trent did not open the abbey, then who did?' asked a puzzled Crabb.

'That is what we have to discover. We now know that it was not just a casual decision to visit the abbey that arose out of the evening's conversation as our suspects claimed. It had already been decided that they would visit the abbey at twelve that evening. Furthermore the stranger who talked with Trent was of a striking resemblance to our friend Jenkins!'

'I see, sir.'

'We have been led a merry dance by these five people, Tom, and no mistake about it. First they cannot remember who suggested the midnight visit to the abbey. Then they claim that the abbey was open upon their arrival there, but we know that Trent never met them there. I am almost certain that some of them at least had met the deceased man before yesterday evening. Hollinger's claim that he visited this Doctor Meadows in Cheltenham is quite clearly a lie, and Anstruther does not appear to be a major in the Guards. I think all five of them came to Tewkesbury to meet one another and to visit the abbey in search of the Templar tomb. For all I know they could have all murdered that poor man and dumped him inside Sir Roger's tomb when they were unexpectedly disturbed by Constable Reynolds. I think it is time, Tom, that we got the truth out of all these people. They are taking us for fools and simpletons — and I for one am rather tired of all their lies and deceit!'

CHAPTER THREE

TEWKESBURY

'Miss Eames, gentlemen, I thank you for your forbearance in this matter.'

It was later that afternoon, and Ravenscroft was standing with his back towards the open fire, facing his five suspects in the snug of the Hop Pole Hotel.

'Most inconsiderate, I say,' muttered Ganniford, glancing at his watch before irritably thrusting the timepiece back into the pocket of his red waistcoat.

'I appreciate that you are all anxious to leave the town at the earliest opportunity and proceed with your respective itineraries—'

'Should have left hours ago. Regimental business to be transacted,' interrupted Major Anstruther grooming his moustache with his fingers.

'—but I have to remind you all that we are dealing with a very serious occurrence,' continued Ravenscroft, wondering whether this latest attempt to discover the truth from the members of his audience would be any more successful than his previous questioning. 'Murder is a crime that cannot be taken lightly.'

'I think we have all told you, Herr Inspector, that this crime has nothing to do with any of us. It was just unfortunate that we came across the open sarcophagus, when we were visiting the abbey,' smiled Hollinger.

'As you say, Doctor, it was just unfortunate that it was you and your companions who discovered the open tomb and not anyone else. You have all stated that none of you had ever met the deceased gentleman before yesterday evening — but I clearly believe that is not the case.'

'Damn it, sir, are you calling us liars!' growled Anstruther. 'Such accusations are unfounded, sir, and cannot go uncontested.'

'I think, Major, that we should allow the inspector to proceed,' offered Miss Eames, seeking to placate her companion.

'Well spoken, my good lady. The sooner we allow the inspector to continue with his investigations, the quicker we may all be permitted to leave,' suggested Jenkins, polishing the lens of his spectacles.

'Thank you, sir. As I said, I believe that the deceased gentleman was known to each and every one of you. In fact, it is highly likely that he was the reason for you all visiting the town in the first place.'

'Ridiculous, man! Never seen the fellow before!' protested Ganniford wriggling uneasily in his chair.

'That is what you all say, but I would ask you all to consider this case from my point of view. I am called to the abbey to investigate the appearance of a recently deceased gentleman in an open tomb; then I learn from my constable that he found all five of you gathered round the sarcophagus at twelve o'clock yesterday evening. You would all agree that this raises certain suspicions. Two questions immediately come to mind — firstly, I ask myself, why were these people visiting the abbey at such a late hour—'

'Told you that man—' interrupted Ganniford.

'Ah yes, you had declared that you had all met for the first time over dinner, and somehow the conversation turned to the abbey, and someone suggested it would be a good idea to go and view the monuments at such a late hour,' continued Ravenscroft, as Crabb took out his pocket-book and licked the end of his pencil.

'That is what happened, Inspector, what is so strange about that?' pronounced Hollinger, with a shrug of his shoulders.

'Quite — but when I questioned each of you earlier today, none of you could agree as to who it was who first suggested the idea. In fact, Dr Hollinger's account of the dinner conversation would seem to differ from that given by everyone else.'

'We cannot remember everything that was said at the dinner table,' emphasized Ganniford.

'Then there is the further question — why was it that five comparative strangers decided to meet up together, on such an inhospitable night, in such a town as Tewkesbury?'

'This is a hotel, man. People stay in such places,' snapped Anstruther.

'And you all have such perfect reasons for being here,' smiled Ravenscroft, warming to his subject. 'Major Anstruther staying here after visiting a lady in Bristol before your return to your regiment in London; Dr Hollinger pausing here for the night after visiting his medical colleague in Cheltenham; Miss Eames seeking solace after the death of her father; and you, Mr Ganniford and Mr Jenkins, taking a respite from your leisurely tour of the Cotswolds and your visit to the spires of Oxford. Such a coincidence that you are all here on the same night, and that you all decided to visit the abbey together at such a late hour.'

'This is all quite ridiculous! You are just going round in circles, man.'

'Ah, Major Anstruther of the Guards. Why is it that there is no record of you being employed in such military activity?'

'Don't know what yer're talking about.'

'Earlier today my constable visited the local library here, where he consulted the Army List for the past three years. He could find no record of your name being included in such a list. How do you explain that, Major?'

'Well — I — I don't. There must be some mistake. Been in the Guards for past thirteen years. Printing error. These things happen all the time. Damn it, you can make enquiries with the regiment if you don't believe me.'

'We certainly will. Then there is you, Dr Hollinger — visiting a colleague, a Dr Meadows in Cheltenham. Well, I have to tell you that no such doctor is to be found in the local directories. How do you explain that?' asked Ravenscroft, sensing the growing unease within the group.

'Simple, my dear Inspector. Doctor Meadows has only just recently taken up residence in the town. Your directory must have been printed before his arrival.'

'Then we have you, Miss Eames. You say you and your late father resided in Ludlow. I have made enquiries with the local station in that town, and thirty minutes ago received a reply from them, by telegram, stating that there is no family of the name of Eames living in the locality. Perhaps you would care to enlighten us, Miss Eames?'

The lady in question turned away abruptly and bought a handkerchief to her eyes.

'Look here, Ravenscroft, what is all this about?' interrupted Ganniford. 'You can see the poor lady is distressed. Totally uncalled for, all this. Smacks of bullying in my book. Shall need to speak with your superiors, Ravenscroft. I suppose you have been checking up on us as well?'

Ravenscroft smiled, realizing that his questioning might at last be on the verge of obtaining the truth.

'Where is all this leading us, Ravenscroft?' asked Jenkins.

'Ah, Mr Jenkins. How did you know that the abbey would be open at such a late hour?'

'We didn't. We just assumed that it would be. If it had been closed, then we would have all have simply returned to the Hop Pole. As it was, we found the building open.'

'That is rather strange. When I visited Trent, the verger, earlier today, he was quite emphatic that he had locked the abbey when he and The Rev'd Jesterson left it at eight that evening,' said Ravenscroft, turning to face the antiquary.

'Well, I suppose that someone had opened it later that evening. There was evidently more than one key,' replied Jenkins, looking away quickly.

'Mr Trent also told me that a gentleman had called upon him at nine that evening offering to pay him to meet him and his companions outside the abbey at twelve that same evening.'

'Well, there you are then, Inspector. That explains why the abbey was open.'

'But Trent did not keep the appointment. He decided to visit his local drinking hostelry instead. However, he has described the gentleman who called upon him, and this man would seem to prove a strong likeness to yourself, Mr Jenkins,' said Ravenscroft with conviction.

'This is quite ridiculous. The man must be mistaken,' protested Jenkins.

'Perhaps my constable should go and fetch Trent? I am sure he would clear up this matter. Constable, if you would be so kind—'

'Oh, for goodness sake, Jenkins, let's tell the man all we know, or we shall all be here for the rest of the week,' snapped Ganniford.

'I think that would be for the best, gentlemen,' said Miss Eames, still dabbing her eyes with her handkerchief.

'That would be most advisable,' said Ravenscroft pausing for a few moments as the various members of the group each sought to avoid his gaze. 'I must inform you all that it is a criminal offence to withhold vital information that may prove essential to the solving of a serious crime.'

'Perhaps I should begin,' offered Hollinger. 'You are correct, Inspector, when you say that we each had a reason for visiting the town — but I also have to inform you that none of us had met each other until yesterday evening, and that we had nothing to do with the death of that man.'

'Please go on,' urged Ravenscroft.

'Oh, I'll tell the inspector,' interrupted Ganniford, in his usual irritable manner.

'As you wish,' said Hollinger shrugging his shoulders.

'Two weeks ago, Stanhope, the fellow we found last night in that tomb, came to my house and showed me a chart that seemed to indicate that I was a descendant of that medieval fellow, Sir Roger Pole, de Pole, or whatever his name was. Said he had spent five years in compiling the chart and tracing the various family lines. At first I thought the man was an idiot, or, worse still, some trickster, and told him to leave, but then he said he had been to see you, Jenkins, and convinced you of the legitimacy of the claim,' said Ganniford turning towards his friend.

'Mr Jenkins, can you confirm this?' enquired Ravenscroft, somewhat confused by this new admission.

'It is certainly true, Inspector; the man had indeed visited me first and, like my good friend Ganniford here, I had at first thought that his information was entirely fabricated, but the more we talked the more convinced I became that I was indeed also a descendant of Sir Roger de la Pole,' replied Jenkins.

'I see,' said Ravenscroft. 'Major?'

'Came to see me about a month ago. Said much the same thing.'

'And you, Doctor?'

'It seems that I too am of the same bloodline,' replied Hollinger.

'I can also confirm that the man was the same one who also visited me and my late father,' added Miss Eames, looking down at the floor nervously.

'So each of you had been approached by the deceased man, who had informed you that you were all descended from the Templar Knight, Sir Roger de la Pole,' said Ravenscroft giving a sideways glance at Crabb.

'I know it all sounds rather peculiar,' muttered Ganniford.

'That is the reason for our being in Tewkesbury yesterday evening,' said Miss Eames looking intently at

Ravenscroft. 'Mr Robarts came to see us in Ludlow, and like the two gentlemen who have just spoken, I was somewhat sceptical of his claims. However, like Mr Ganniford and Mr Jenkins, I became convinced that the man was genuine. He thought it would be an excellent idea if we all met together in Tewkesbury, as we were all related to each other. Last week I received a letter from the gentleman, telling me to travel to Tewkesbury where I would meet similar persons as myself.'

'And did all of you receive such a letter?' asked Ravenscroft, relieved that at last the truth was being revealed.

'Exactly the same. Told us to meet outside the abbey door at twelve last night,' said Ganniford.

'Forgive me, gentlemen and lady, but I find it rather strange that each of you, after meeting this one man only once before, should have been so willing to leave your respective homes, to travel to Tewkesbury and to meet a group of strangers outside the abbey at such a late hour,' said a bewildered Ravenscroft.

'Told you, we should have kept it to ourselves,' snapped Anstruther. 'I knew the man would never believe us.'

'Did this gentleman give any reason why you were all to journey to Tewkesbury?'

A long pause followed Ravenscroft's question, during which Ganniford moved uneasily in his chair, and Miss Eames played nervously with the handkerchief in her lap, as the three remaining members either stared out of the window or down at the floor. Crabb coughed before letting out a deep sigh.

'I will repeat my question — what was the reason for your journey to Tewkesbury?' asked Ravenscroft, becoming frustrated by the apparent abrupt end to his new line of enquiry.

'Our instructions were to meet together outside the abbey at twelve o'clock,' replied a reluctant Ganniford.

'For what purpose?'

'To meet with our host, and to seek out the last resting place of our ancestor, Sir Roger de la Pole. That is all,' added Hollinger emphatically.

'I see,' said Ravenscroft turning away, deep in thought.

'So you see, there was nothing sinister in our meeting. None of us was to know that the fellow was already dead inside that tomb,' said Ganniford.

'Now you know the reason for our meeting together, Ravenscroft, perhaps you will allow us all to leave and go our own separate ways,' said Anstruther rising from his seat.

'I too have an urgent need to return to London,' added Hollinger.

'You must see, Inspector that none of us was in any way involved with the poor man's demise,' implored Miss Eames. 'None of us would have had any reason to see him dead.'

'I am sorry that we cannot be of any further assistance to you, Inspector,' said Jenkins, rising to his feet.

'I'm afraid I cannot let any of you leave,' announced Ravenscroft.

'Oh, for goodness sake, man! We've told you why we all came here, and how we found the man,' protested Anstruther pacing up and down the room.

'I can see how you came to the town yesterday and why you were asked to meet together outside the abbey — it would have been easier for you all, and for our investigation, if you had all told us the truth when first questioned.'

'I am sorry for that, Inspector Ravenscroft,' said Miss Eames.

'I know it looks bad, but to tell you the truth we were all a bit put out finding that fellow like that in that tomb; then your constable came on us unexpected, and we all thought it would be better if we tried to make it look like an accident, us all meeting like that,' said Ganniford. 'Sorry for all the mix up. No hard feelings like.'

Ravenscroft turned away and looked out of the window. What had looked like an encouraging line of new enquiry seemed to be disappearing rapidly.

'Well, if you will excuse us,' said Hollinger, after a few moments of silence had elapsed.

'Tell you something, Ravenscroft, there was that fellow Ross. You might do better having a word with him,' said Ganniford, easing himself from out of his chair.

'Ross? I do not understand,' said a bewildered Ravenscroft turning round once more to face the group.

'Yes, of course, Mr Ross,' said Miss Eames.

'I had almost forgotten him,' interjected Hollinger. 'You see, Inspector, there were six of us there that night.'

'Do please go on,' asked Ravenscroft his curiosity aroused.

'When we all met up at the abbey, we were debating whether we should enter the building or not, when the man called Ross suddenly arrived,' began Ganniford.

'We assumed that he was another of our group,' added Jenkins.

'Did this man Ross go into the abbey with you?' enquired Ravenscroft.

'Yes, he was the first to enter the building, now I come to remember,' said Ganniford. 'We naturally followed him inside hoping that our host Stanhope would be there waiting to meet us, but, of course, there was no sign of the fellow.'

'And what happened to this Mr Ross? My constable said there were only five of you standing there round the tomb,' said Ravenscroft.

'That's the funny thing, shortly after we entered the abbey we lost track of him. Deuce funny thing. Never saw him again,' added Anstruther.

'He's the fellow you should be questioning, not us,' interjected Ganniford. 'He was acting in a decidedly suspicious manner if you ask me.'

'I see. What can you tell me about this man Ross? How old was he? What did he look like? Did he say anything which might enable my constable and I to locate him?'

'I suppose he was about thirty in years, what you say, of tall stature, black hair,' offered Hollinger.

'He did say he lived near Bredon, but that he originated from Kirkintilloch, in Scotland, I think that is what he told us,' offered Miss Eames.

'You have a remarkable memory,' said Ganniford.

'That's who your murderer was! Obviously killed the man before we got to the abbey, and once he knew we were all inside he slipped away again, knowing suspicion would fall on us,' announced Anstruther.

'I do not think we can assume that, Major, until I have had an opportunity to question this man Ross. My constable and I will certainly make enquiries regarding the said gentleman. However one other matter is puzzling me. Miss Eames, you stated a moment ago that the man who visited you was called Robarts, yet I thought that the man's name was Stanhope according to you Mr Ganniford. Perhaps you would enlighten me?'

'Well, yes, that's the odd thing. The man seems to have called himself by a different name when he visited each of us in turn,' said Ganniford, reluctantly, after a moment's unease.

'I can confirm, Inspector, that the man did indeed call himself Robarts,' offered Miss Eames.

'Called himself Grantly when he visited me,' muttered Anstruther.

'Make a note of these names, Crabb,' instructed Ravenscroft.

'Robarts, Grantly and Stanhope,' said a studious Crabb writing in his pocket book.

'Said his name was Thorne,' said Hollinger.

'Mr Jenkins?' asked Ravenscroft.

'Gave his name as Harding,' answered the antiquary, shaking his head.

'Thorne. Harding,' muttered Crabb without looking up from his book.

'Interesting. Thank you, Miss Eames, gentlemen. My constable and I will endeavour to track down and question Mr Ross. Until he has confirmed your account of last night's events, I am afraid I must ask you all to remain here,' said Ravenscroft, knowing that his words would prove unpopular with some members of the group.

'Look here, Ravenscroft, this just won't do,' protested Anstruther.

'When do you propose speaking with this Ross?' asked Jenkins.

'You say he resided near Bredon. My constable will consult the local directories and once we have confirmed his place of residence, we will endeavour to question the gentleman first thing in the morning. It is rather late in the day to travel over there now. If you would all meet me in here tomorrow at twelve, I would be most obliged.'

'Confound it, sir, this won't do at all!' grumbled Anstruther.

'I agree with the inspector,' interjected Jenkins, seeking to bring calm to the situation. 'I think we can all appreciate that Mr Ravenscroft has his duty to perform. A most terrible murder has been perpetrated. It is our duty assist the police with their inquiries.'

'Thank you, Mr Jenkins,' nodded Ravenscroft.

'Suppose it is rather late in the day. We shall just have to spend another night in this dreary little town,' said Ganniford, shrugging his shoulders, before sinking back into his armchair.

'I for one am happy to comply with the inspector's wishes,' added Miss Eames smiling.

'Insufferable!' muttered Anstruther as he strode out of the room.

'You must not mind the major. When he has calmed down I am sure he will come round to your way of thinking. I will ensure he complies with your wishes,' said Hollinger.

'I thank you all. Until tomorrow then at twelve.'

CHAPTER FOUR

LEDBURY AND BREDON'S NORTON

'Well, my dear, it seems that I am faced with a mystery that may prove somewhat difficult to solve.'

Ravenscroft was sitting with his wife, later that evening, before a roaring fire in their small house in Church Lane.

'I am sure you and Tom will be able to find a solution,' replied Lucy, sympathetically.

'I am afraid I cannot share your optimism, my dear,' said Ravenscroft, somewhat gloomily. 'It might have been wiser to have said that I was indisposed; taken ill with a serious ailment, or broken a leg, confined to bed for the rest of the month. Tom could have made my excuses. Then they would have sent someone out from either Worcester or Gloucester, to take charge of the case. I am sure they would have more success than I have had so far. We would then have been free to have undertaken our excursion to London.'

'You know you would never have done that. You are far too conscientious to neglect your duty. Now, tell me more about your case. It all sounds very mysterious — five strangers meeting for the first time outside the doors of Tewkesbury Abbey at twelve o'clock at night, looking for their supposed ancestor, Sir Roger de la Pole, and then finding that man dead inside one of the tombs. It all sounds like something out of a novel by Mary Shelley or Mr Stevenson.'

'I must admit that it does all sound rather Gothic. I really cannot believe that five supposedly intelligent strangers would all journey to Tewkesbury to meet one another just because some man had told them all that they are descendants of a Templar Knight. No, I think something else must have bought them to the abbey. They were looking for something that was connected with Sir Roger — and whatever it was, must have been inside that empty tomb.'

'And what about your mysterious Mr Ross? Now he appears to be very interesting, I must say. He seems like someone right out of *Jane Eyre* or *Wuthering Heights*.'

'What a vivid imagination you have, my dear! But, yes, you are correct. He does appear briefly outside the abbey one minute, enters the building the next moment and is seen no more. Tom has been able to locate a Charles Ross, who is apparently living in some village with the strange sounding name of Bredon's Norton.'

'Wherever is that?'

'Near Bredon Hill, the other side of Tewkesbury and Pershore, I believe. Tom and I must make an early start in the morning to seek out this man. Perhaps this fellow Ross holds the key to this mystery. Another thing I cannot quite comprehend — the deceased stranger seems to have used a different name when he visited each of the five suspects. Now why would he do that?'

'Perhaps he wanted to make sure that no one would know that he had visited all five of your people. What names did he use?' asked Lucy her curiosity aroused.

'Nothing so common as your Smith or Jones. Stanhope, Harding, Robarts, Thorne and Grantly, I think. Yes, that was it. Such an odd collection of surnames. You could not invent such names if you tried. Why use those names?'

'Stanhope, Harding, Thorne. Ah, I think I may have solved your mystery. Go through the names again,' laughed Lucy.

'Stanhope, Robarts, Harding, Thorne and Grantly,' repeated Ravenscroft looking perplexed.

'Your deceased stranger was either a man of great literary tendencies, or had a remarkable sense of humour,' smiled Lucy.

'Tell me more; I am intrigued.'

'Stanhope, Robarts, Harding, Thorne and Grantly are all characters in the Barsetshire novels of Mr Anthony Trollope.'

'Really? How clever you are to have worked that out.'

'I remember reading most of the books when I was younger,' said Lucy, smiling. 'If I recall, your five characters are mainly clerical gentlemen.'

'What a strange state of affairs. Why go to such elaborate lengths to conceal your true identity? I cannot see the reason for such deception when a straightforward Smith or Jones would have been sufficient. With your powers of deduction, my dear, I see that I will have to enrol you in the local constabulary. With you by my side we will be able to solve our crimes in half the time,' said Ravenscroft, rising from his chair.

'Now you are being patronizing, Samuel,' teased Lucy.

'That I would never dare to do! You are far too shrewd to see through any kind of flattery that I might be foolish enough to attempt. Anthony Trollope, you say. Now there is a mystery all in itself. But we have sat here long enough, my dear. Time for bed; an early start beckons in the morning if Tom and I are to seek out this fellow Ross in Bredon's Norton.'

* * *

They had begun their journey that morning from Ledbury to Bredon in warm March sunshine and under a clear blue sky, but once their trap had crossed the Severn and skirted the town of Tewkesbury, a fleet of ominous black clouds began to drift quickly across the empty space above their heads.

'How much further, Tom?' asked Ravenscroft, as their vehicle made its way through the quiet sleepy village of Bredon.

'Only another two or three miles, sir, according to the map,' replied Crabb.

'I shall be glad when we get there. I fear it will not be long before the heavens will open up on us. The hill in front of us over there certainly looks dark and forbidding,' said Ravenscroft, turning up the collar of his coat, as he contemplated the events of the previous two days.

Why had five complete strangers decided to meet one another for the first time outside the abbey on such a cold wet evening? They had each claimed that they had been summoned to seek out the tomb of their ancient ancestor, but instead they had found the body of the man who had arranged their meeting. At first they had sought to conceal the truth from him, and although he had eventually been successful in his questioning, he still knew that there was much more to unravel, more admissions to be made, before the mystery of the deceased man could be solved. But all that could wait until he had pursued his present line of inquiry.

Then there was the murdered man found lying inside the old Templar tomb. Why had he called himself by so many different names? And why had he chosen the novels of Anthony Trollope as his source of inspiration? The man had obviously been well read, but was there something more behind that choice?

Now they were on their way to seek out the sixth member of the group, the man known as Ross, who had made but a fleeting brief appearance at the abbey before disappearing into the darkness once more. Was he also a descendant of the crusader knight — and, if so, why had he been so anxious to quit the scene? At least he had left some information behind him, and the directory had given the name Mr Charles Ross of Bredon's Norton. Perhaps the man might provide them with some valuable information concerning the death of the stranger — or he might well prove to be the murderer himself.

'I think we go off the road here,' said Crabb, turning the trap sharply to the right. 'Map says the track runs up to the hill to Bredon's Norton; there is no other way through.'

As they made their way along the old rutty way, waves of mist suddenly descended and drifted ahead of them, quickly engulfing them with their vapour and seeking to impede the horse's progress.

'Go slower, Tom, we don't know what is ahead. I can hardly see anything in front of us. I've never seen the weather change so quickly. This horrible damp mist seems to cling to one. Extraordinary. I don't think I have ever been so cold in my life before,' said Ravenscroft, coughing, rubbing his hands together for warmth and wishing he had chosen a different day for their expedition.

'I've never seen mist as thick as this before. We used to have a lot of them on the farm when I was a child, but nothing so clammy and dark as this. There now, easy, boy!' said Crabb pulling up the horse sharply. 'Easy there! Don't think he cares much for it either.'

'I think I can see a light from over there. Must be coming from a building,' said Ravenscroft, pointing through the thick fog. 'It is more like the middle of the night than early morning. Leave the horse here, Tom. You can tie him up to that tree.'

The two men dismounted from their vehicle and, after Crabb had said a few words of reassurance to the animal, they made their way slowly towards the faltering light.

'I think it's a farm or house of some kind,' said Ravenscroft, buttoning the top of his coat tighter as they drew near. 'I think I can just make out a light above the doorway. Let's knock the door and see if its occupants can tell us if Ross lives here or nearby.'

Ravenscroft lifted the old rusty knocker and, as he bought it down on the thick oak door, it seemed as though the sound seemed to echo into the stillness of the strange landscape in which they had found themselves.

'Not at home,' remarked Crabb, after a few moments had passed.

'You might be right. Let us try again—' But before Ravenscroft could repeat his action, the door suddenly opened to reveal a tall, thin, middle-aged man holding a candlestick in one hand.

'Good day, sir. We are looking for Mr Charles Ross,' said Ravenscroft, noting that the occupier was dressed entirely in black.

'I'm Ross,' replied the man, in what Ravenscroft thought to be a Scottish accent.

'Thank goodness for that. I thought we had lost our way in this fog. My name is Detective Inspector Ravenscroft and this is my assistant, Constable Crabb. I would be obliged if you would give us a few minutes of your time.'

The man frowned and stared at them; then, without speaking, he pushed open the door further and indicated that the two men were to enter.

'Thank you, sir,' said Ravenscroft, stepping into the large room, which appeared to be sparsely furnished with an oak table and two wooden dining chairs. A large candelabra situated in the middle of the table emitted a flickering, faltering light from its three candles, and the remains of a nearly burnt-out log fought for the last moments of its life in the ash-strewn hearth.

The man closed the creaking door behind them. Although Ravenscroft had left the darkness and clinging mist behind him, he felt no warmer in the cold, uninviting room.

'What can I do for you, gentlemen?' asked their host.

'Could you tell me where you were the evening before last?' asked Ravenscroft.

'Why?'

'If you could just answer the question, Mr Ross, I would be most obliged.'

'I was here, as I always am.'

'We have reason to believe that you were in Tewkesbury. You were seen going into the abbey at twelve in the evening.'

'I may have been,' said Ross, giving a loud cough before turning away to poke the expiring log in the hearth with a brass poker.

'We understand that you met five other persons outside the abbey.'

Their host said nothing as he continued with his task.

'I must tell you that I am investigating the death of a stranger whose body was found in one of the tombs, which had been violated inside the abbey. We know that you and five other people entered the abbey and discovered the deceased, but that you disappeared before my constable took charge of the situation. Why was that, Mr Ross?'

'I could see no point in remaining there.'

'So you admit that you were in Tewkesbury on Tuesday evening?'

'If you know all this, why ask me?' grumbled Ross, laying down the poker.

'May I ask the reason for your visit?' persisted Ravenscroft.

'I suppose you have spoken to the others?'

'Yes.'

'Then they would have told you the reason for our visit.'

'To seek out the tomb of Sir Roger de la Pole. Can we assume, Mr Ross, that you are also a descendant of the knight?'

'You can assume what you like,' replied Ross, coughing again as he turned away and gazed out of the window.

'Can you tell me the name of the gentleman who called upon you with this information?'

'He said his name was Crosbie.'

Ravenscroft gave Crabb a smile. Probably Crosbie was yet another alias used by the deceased man and no doubt another creation of Anthony Trollope. 'And what did this gentleman say to you?'

'He claimed that I was a descendant of the Templar. I did not believe a word of it, of course.'

'Oh, why was that, sir?'

'I could see the man was a charlatan.'

'But you still made the journey to the abbey.'

'My curiosity was aroused. I wanted to see what the mountebank was up to.'

'Did you see inside the tomb?' asked Ravenscroft, annoyed that the man Ross was going to great lengths not to face his questioner.

'Of course.'

'And you can identify the body as the man Crosbie who called upon you.'

'I can.'

'Did you discover the open tomb before the other members of the party?'

'I might have done.'

'And why did you not stay with the rest of the group?'

Ross shrugged his shoulders and turned briefly in Ravenscroft's direction, before gazing out of the window once more.

'Mr Ross, I do not see why you kept the appointment at the abbey, if you believed that the man Crosbie was some kind of fraudster,' asked Ravenscroft, anxious to know more of the Scotsman's real motives.

'I told you, I was curious to know what the man was about,' coughed Ross, turning his back on the detective once more.

'And what was he "about"?'

'I don't know. I never had the chance to ask him, as he was dead. I've answered all your questions. Now if that will be all, I have plenty of things to attend to.'

'Mr Ross, I do not think you have been entirely forthcoming with us,' protested Ravenscroft, determined that his visit should not have been in vain.

'I've told you all I know.'

'But I don't think you have, Mr Ross. I believe you arrived at the abbey first, met the stranger Crosbie, that you both forced open the tomb, and that you then killed your companion before making your way out of the abbey—'

'Nonsense, man!' retorted Ross, glaring at Ravenscroft. 'If I had killed the man, as you suggest, why would I have then returned to the abbey when the others arrived?'

'You tell me Mr Ross.'

'I've told you, I arrived at the abbey just after the others. I was late because I had just ridden all the way through the rain from here to Tewkesbury.'

'It must have been a terrible journey for you,' remarked Crabb.

'We Scots are used to the bad weather.'

'I still do not see why you and five other intelligent people would make all this effort to travel to a town which none of you appear ever to have visited before, just because some stranger had told you all that you were all descendants of a medieval Templar Knight. What were you all really after, Mr Ross? What really bought you all to Tewkesbury? Was it something inside that tomb that you were all seeking?'

'I have told you all I know.'

'I am determined to discover the truth, and if you cannot provide me with the answers I require, I am afraid I will have no recourse but to take you into custody. Crabb, the cuffs, if you will.'

'You cannot do that, man,' protested Ross.

'I think you will find that I can,' replied Ravenscroft firmly.

'All right, Ravenscroft, I suppose you will not let this matter rest until I tell you all that I know. The man told me that there was a goblet,' sighed Ross.

'Go on, sir,' said Ravenscroft, hoping that at last he was about to learn the truth.

'The man Crosbie showed me a document which he said was the last will and testament of Sir Roger de la Pole. Apparently whilst on the crusades in Jerusalem he had acquired a valuable goblet of some kind, made of gold, encrusted with rich stones, and had bought it back to Tewkesbury with him. The paper said that the goblet had been hidden but that it could be claimed by any of his descendants who could find it,' replied Ross, somewhat reluctantly.

'I see,' said Ravenscroft.

'All sounds a bit farfetched, if you ask me,' uttered Crabb looking up from his pocket book.

'That was exactly my own thought, Constable. The whole thing sounded a complete fabrication invented by an overjealous criminal mind.'

'So that's what enticed everyone to meet outside the abbey,' said Ravenscroft. 'The promise of the discovery of a medieval jewel-encrusted goblet.'

'I did not believe a word of it, of course. As I said before, I just wanted to see what the charlatan was up to,' added Ross.

'Tell me, sir, did this Mr Crosbie ever extract any money from you during your meeting with him?'

'No. There was never any talk of money or payment.'

'I see. Did Crosbie give any indication as to where this supposed gold goblet was likely to be found?' asked Ravenscroft.

'None — but he believed we might discover its whereabouts if we located the tomb of Sir Roger in the abbey. He believed that the tomb might provide us with some kind of clue as to where the goblet was to be found. It was all nonsense, of course.'

'As you say, Mr Ross, all nonsense, and yet five other people seem to have believed in this so-called nonsense.'

'That was their business. Now, I have told you all that I know.'

'Thank you, Mr Ross. I will now be returning to Tewkesbury to have words with the other five people, to see if they can add anything to what you have told us. I would be greatly obliged if you would accompany us there.'

'Whatever for, Inspector? I've told you all I know,' protested Ross.

'It is important to our investigations that I speak to all six of you together, and that the others are able to confirm your story,' urged Ravenscroft.

'I don't really see—'

'I have to remind you, sir, that a murder has taken place, and I have reason to believe that the outrage can only have been committed by one of your party. It is imperative that you return with us now to Tewkesbury,' said Ravenscroft, raising his voice, as Crabb coughed and took a step forward in Ross's direction.

'Very well then. If you two gentlemen would give me a minute or two to change my clothes and prepare for the journey,' said the Scotsman, reluctantly.

'Of course, sir. My constable and I will wait outside for you,' said Ravenscroft turning away and walking towards the door.

* * *

'Well, sir, do you believe all that nonsense about the gold goblet?' asked Crabb as he and his superior made their way back to the waiting horse and trap.

'To tell you the truth, Tom, I don't know quite what to think. If Ross is telling us the truth, then that would explain why the six members of our group all decided to keep their appointment with the mysterious Crosbie, Stanhope, or whatever his real name was, outside the abbey. Each one of them must have thought that they would be able to find the goblet. The prospect of obtaining riches would have bought them all to Tewkesbury.'

'Or curiosity?'

'Indeed. Like Ross, one, or all of them, probably realized that the whole fantastic thing was a giant hoax, and yet were determined to see what the eventual outcome would be. Still it seems rather a long journey for them to have made just to satisfy their curiosity.'

'Ross could have just made the whole thing up,' suggested Crabb.

'He could have done, in which case this whole goblet story is pure invention. That is why I was so insistent that he accompany us back to Tewkesbury. Once he tells his account before the others, we can then confront them with the story and see what their reactions are. If the story is true, at least then we will know what was the real motive for the murder.'

'Do you think that goblet could have been inside the tomb?'

'That may be so, in which case one of the group may have met the deceased man earlier in the evening, and together they raised the lid of the sarcophagus, and finding that neither of them was able to reach the goblet, the deceased man climbed in, handed the item to our killer, who then decided to keep it for himself. After killing the unfortunate Crosbie, and finding that he could not replace the stone slab, our killer then made sure that he kept his appointment with the others, thereby ensuring that they would all discover the body together and avoid suspicion falling upon himself.'

'It all sounds all very neat, sir, but you keep saying "him". Can I take it then that you are discounting Miss Eames from your list of suspects?' asked Crabb.

'Not at all. We know that the slab could not be moved by one man on his own, but I have no doubt that it could be moved by a man and woman together. Any one of our group could have been the killer.'

'My money is on Ross. Don't like him at all. I thought he was rather a shifty-looking character — and what a strange miserable place to live in.'

'I agree with you. I don't think I have set foot in such a wretched, cold, uninviting room as that one. No wonder Ross has such a hacking cough. How anyone can live there I do not know. There was hardly a stick of furniture in the room, and as for that fire, well it had clearly been dying for days. I can't say I took to our host either. There was a strange coldness about the man that I found unsettling. Did you notice how he avoided answering any of my questions directly? It was as though he did not want us to look into his eyes. Clearly he has more to tell us. But to return to Sir Roger. If Ross's story is true, then the goblet, or something else of value, must have been inside that tomb. However, we may be getting ahead of ourselves and letting our imaginations run wild. There may be no gold goblet at all. We still have to make our way back to Tewkesbury and confront the others. Where the devil is that fellow Ross? He seems to be taking rather a long time in preparing himself for our journey.'

'You don't think he has changed his mind, sir?'

Ravenscroft looked at Crabb, then both of them ran quickly back towards the house.

'The door is open,' said Ravenscroft stepping into the room once more and calling out.

'No answer, sir.'

'There is another room off this one. Perhaps he is in there.'

'I'll take a look,' said Crabb, entering the other chamber. 'Nothing there, sir, only an old bed.'

'Then Ross must have slipped out of the house when we were not looking.'

'I think we would have seen him,' said Crabb, returning to the main room.

'Well, he does not appear to be here. I agree with you. I was sure that we were facing the house all the time and would have seen him had he left the building.'

'It must have been the fog, sir.'

'Damn it, Crabb, we should have secured him while we could. How foolish of us to have let him slip through our fingers,' said an annoyed Ravenscroft.

'We could take a look outside.'

'No point. The fog is too thick — and we have no indication as to which way he may have gone. Our Mr Ross clearly had no intention of accompanying us.'

'What now, sir?'

'There is nothing else for it — we must return to Tewkesbury as soon as possible, and confront our suspects with the story of the missing gold goblet. It will be interesting to see what they have to say.'

CHAPTER FIVE

TEWKESBURY

'Well, Crabb, let us see what our five friends have to say for themselves, when we confront them with this goblet story,' said Ravenscroft, as he and his constable pushed open the door of the Hop Pole.

'Pity we couldn't have bought along that Ross character,' replied Crabb.

'Ross can wait. We can easily return there once we have uncovered the truth about this affair.'

As the two men entered the main room of the inn, Ravenscroft observed that only Jenkins, Ganniford and Miss Eames were present. 'Gentlemen, Miss Eames, forgive the lateness of our arrival. Unfortunately the weather was inclement out near Bredon and our departure was somewhat delayed.'

'And did you find this Ross fellow?' enquired Ganniford in his usual forthright manner, coming forward to meet them.

'We did indeed, and he was able to assist us greatly in our enquiries,' replied Ravenscroft, observing that Ganniford gave his friend a quick sideways glance.

'Has Mr Ross returned with you, Mr Ravenscroft?' asked Miss Eames eagerly.

'Alas, no; Mr Ross seems to have had another appointment,' smiled Ravenscroft.

'Well, there you are then. Told you the fellow was suspicious. You should have arrested him straight away, while you had the chance,' muttered Ganniford squeezing his frame once more into the leather armchair before the fire.

'Do you happen to know whether Dr Hollinger and Major Anstruther are going to join us?' enquired Ravenscroft, seeking to ignore the previous remark.

'Deuce if I know where they are,' proclaimed Ganniford reaching out with his boot to prod the edge of one of the logs that was slumbering in the hearth.

'I'm afraid we have not seen either of the two gentlemen in question this morning,' offered Jenkins.

'Crabb, go and find the rooms in which these two gentlemen reside, and if they are there, ask them to join us if you will,' instructed Ravenscroft.

'Very well, sir.'

'So, what did this Ross say to you?' asked Ganniford after the constable had left the room.

'Mr Ross was quite forthcoming, but I would rather wait until we are all present, Mr Ganniford,' replied Ravenscroft, seating himself in one of the armchairs.

'Do you think it will be possible, Inspector, for us to leave after you have informed us of the details of your visit to Mr Ross?' asked Jenkins. 'We would appreciate it if you would allow us to catch the afternoon train back to London.'

'I cannot say, sir, whether that will be possible at this stage.'

'Insufferable,' uttered Ganniford, turning away with a look of disdain.

The four occupants of the room sat in silence for some minutes, listening to the grandfather clock ticking in the corner and watching the logs burning in the hearth.

'I think you had better come quickly, sir,' said a breathless, ashen-faced Crabb suddenly entering the room.

Ravenscroft took one look at his constable and sprang to his feet.

'Whatever is the matter?' asked Ganniford, struggling to raise himself from his seat.

'This way, sir,' said Crabb.

'We will come with you,' said Jenkins.

'I think it would be better if the lady and gentlemen remained here,' blurted out an anxious Crabb.

'Look here, if there is something afoot—' began Ganniford.

'I'm afraid I must insist that you all remain here,' said Ravenscroft firmly. 'I can assure you that we will return as soon as possible.'

'Up the stairs to Number Five, sir,' said Crabb, leading the way along the corridor. 'It's Dr Hollinger. Something terrible has happened to him! I'm afraid it's not a pleasant sight.'

The two men ran up the stairs, Ravenscroft nearly colliding with the chambermaid on the landing, before Crabb pushed open one of the bedroom doors.

'Good God!' exclaimed Ravenscroft looking down at the bloodstained sheets on the bed. 'Hollinger. Someone has stabbed Hollinger!'

'I came as soon as I found him,' said Crabb, recoiling into the corner of the room and bringing a pocket handkerchief up to his nose.

'Quickly — lock the door, Tom. We don't want anyone else coming in here,' said Ravenscroft, approaching the bed and gently pulling back the blood-soaked upper sheet. 'What a mess. It looks as though Hollinger has been stabbed at least three times in the chest and stomach.'

'Terrible business, sir.'

'Why on earth would anyone want to do this to poor Hollinger? I cannot understand why he has been killed like this. Look around the floor, Crabb, and see if you can find a knife, or anything of a similar nature.'

'Terrible,' muttered a mesmerized Crabb staring down at the corpse.

'Tom, look for a weapon,' repeated Ravenscroft firmly, anxious that his subordinate should be fully occupied.

'Yes, sir,' replied Crabb quickly turning away and beginning the search.

'Whoever killed Hollinger certainly wanted to make sure that he was dead. I would say that he was killed several hours ago, probably during the night, by the state of this congealed blood,' said Ravenscroft peering over the body. 'There is not much sign of a struggle, and the furniture is not disturbed, which would suggest that he was killed whilst he was asleep.'

'Here it is, sir,' said Crabb, holding up a large bloodstained knife. 'It was on the floor in the corner.'

'Our killer must have thrown it there, after he had used it to kill poor Hollinger,' said Ravenscroft taking the knife from Crabb and examining the blade. 'It certainly is a nasty item, Tom. Not the kind of knife used by either a butcher or surgeon. More like an old army knife, I would think. Let us take a further look round the room and see what we can find. Ah, see here, Tom, bloodstained water! Our killer poured out some water from the jug into the bowl and then washed his hands after committing the deed. Ah, yes, and here is the towel he then wiped them on. There are traces of blood on it. I think our murderer was anxious that his hands would be clean in case he encountered anyone outside the room upon his departure.'

'What about his clothes?' asked Crabb.

'I would have thought there would certainly have been blood on his clothing. As the killer stabbed downwards, and then repeated his action a further two times, withdrawing the knife each time, some of the blood would probably have spurted upwards. If he did not want to run the risk of possibly meeting someone outside the room whilst effecting his escape, then he would have either discarded the bloodstained clothes in here, or attempted to have cleaned them before he left.'

'There are some clothes on the chair over here,' said Crabb.

'Almost certainly Hollinger's. Neatly folded and no stains on them,' said Ravenscroft, drawing the sheet over the bloody corpse before crossing over the room to examine the clothing. 'And there are his expensive pocket watch and spectacles on the bedside cabinet. As they have not been taken, I think we can safely conclude that whoever killed Hollinger did not commit such a terrible deed to acquire his valuables. It looks as though our killer must have washed away any surplus blood off his own clothes, before he left the room — unless of course he was staying in the inn and knew that his own room was but a short distance away, either next door, or in close proximity along the same landing. Do we know which rooms our four other suspects occupy?'

'I took the liberty of asking the man downstairs before I came up here. Ganniford occupies the next room on the left-hand side, then Jenkins, with Major Anstruther on the other side. Miss Eames apparently has a room on the lower floor.'

'So it would have been easy for either Ganniford, Jenkins or Anstruther to have slipped out of this room unnoticed and quickly enter their own room. It would have been more difficult for Miss Eames.'

'Surely you cannot suspect her of such a vicious act?' asked Crabb. 'She is too quiet and unassuming to be such a killer.'

'Appearances can sometimes be deceptive. Some of the most terrible unholy killers in history have been women. If Hollinger was fast asleep, it would not have taken much for a woman to have brought down the knife on him, and the quick succession of the second and third blows would have made sure that he had no time to defend himself. I would say that it was probably the first blow that went close to the poor man's heart.'

'Hollinger would have known nothing,' said a subdued Crabb, shaking his head.

'Probably better that way, although who can say what agonies could sweep over one in the moment of death? We must also consider Ross.'

'Ross?'

'Yes, Ross. He could have returned here in the middle of last night, crept into the bedroom, killed Hollinger and then made sure of his escape in the darkness. Had he been wearing a cape or other kind of outer garment, he could have removed it before killing Hollinger, then used it to conceal his blood-spattered clothes. At the moment, however, that is all conjecture. We have no evidence against anyone,' said Ravenscroft, turning away from the blood-soaked bed.

'Ghastly business,' added Crabb.

'We are missing one thing in all this, Tom — where is Major Anstruther?'

'I did not go to his room. I came here first.'

'Then I think we should go there now, before we proceed any further.'

'You don't think that he has also been killed?' asked Crabb, with a look of alarm.

'I don't know what to think, Tom,' interrupted Ravenscroft. 'Lock the door behind you as we leave. We do not want any of the others coming in here.'

The two men closed the door behind them and made their way to the room next door.

Ravenscroft tapped on the wood and, receiving no reply, attempted to force open the door. 'Locked. Go and get someone to open it. I don't want to make a disturbance by forcing the door.'

Crabb quickly disappeared from view, leaving his superior officer to contemplate the events of the past few minutes. Hollinger's sudden death was the last thing he had expected, and Ravenscroft was now forced to accept that the doctor's killing had changed the whole complexion of the case. He had expected to confront his five suspects with Ross's account of the golden goblet. Now he was faced with another murder enquiry. Worse still, he was apprehensive as to what might be found the other side of the closed door.

'Ah there you are. We need you to open this door for us,' instructed Ravenscroft when Crabb returned with the innkeeper.

'This is rather unusual, sir,' protested the man.

'This is police business. Kindly open the door for us.'

The man turned the key in the lock.

'Thank you. You may go now. You can leave this to us,' said Ravenscroft, his hand on the door handle, anxious not to open the door until the owner had departed.

The man gave them a worried look before making his way down the stairs.

'Right. I'll go in first,' said Ravenscroft slowly opening the door. A hesitant, nervous Crabb followed him into the room. 'Empty! No one here. Anstruther must have left and locked the door behind him.'

'Look, sir, on the floor,' said Crabb, pointing to some garments in the corner of the room.

Ravenscroft knelt down and picked up a shirt and pair of trousers. 'See the bloodstains. The shirt in particular is well covered. Our murderer must have been wearing these when he killed Hollinger. See if you can find anything else that might have belonged to Anstruther.'

'Nothing else here, sir,' said Crabb, after searching round the room.

'Exactly as I would have expected. It looks as though Anstruther killed Hollinger, after which he discarded his blood-soaked clothes, before changing into new apparel. He then appears to have then left, taking all his luggage with him.'

'So it was Anstruther who killed Hollinger. He probably killed the man in the coffin as well.'

Ravenscroft said nothing as he walked round the room, examining the rest of its contents with interest. Crabb stood still wondering what course of action his superior officer would now embark upon.

'There is nothing else here of interest,' said Ravenscroft presently. 'We need to know what time Hollinger and Anstruther retired last night, and whether anyone saw the major leaving. I'll go and break the news of Hollinger's death to our three remaining suspects, whilst you go to the mortuary and ask them to come and collect Hollinger's body.'

* * *

'Well, what's happened?' asked an agitated Ganniford, as Ravenscroft returned to the downstairs room.

'I'm afraid I have some rather bad news concerning Dr Hollinger—' began Ravenscroft.

'Oh no!' exclaimed Miss Eames, drawing her hand quickly to her face.

'Here, take a seat, my dear lady,' said Ganniford steering the lady in the direction of one of the armchairs.

'I have to tell you all that we have just found Doctor Hollinger dead in his bedroom. He appears to have been cruelly stabbed.'

Miss Eames let out a cry, as Ganniford took hold of her arm and eased his charge into the chair.

'Stabbbed to death you say?' said a stunned Jenkins.

'I'm afraid so.'

'And Major Anstruther?' asked the antiquary.

'There is no sign of the major in his room. He appears to have left some time ago.'

'You don't think the major killed poor Dr Hollinger?' asked a tearful Miss Eames.

'There, there now, Miss Eames. Do not distress yourself, my dear lady,' said Ganniford trying to sound as comforting as he could.

'My constable has gone to fetch assistance. In the meantime, I must ask each of you when you last saw the doctor and the major.'

'We all had dinner together last night, then afterwards we sat in the snug drinking,' offered Jenkins, recovering his composure and speaking in his usual matter-of-fact voice, before removing his spectacles and cleaning them on his handkerchief.

'And after that?' asked Ravenscroft.

'I retired at around ten,' said a tearful Miss Eames.

'I left shortly afterwards — about ten-thirty,' offered Ganniford.

'Mr Jenkins?' asked Ravenscroft.

'I retired just before eleven. I left the major and the doctor talking together down here.'

'Do you happen to recall what the two gentlemen were talking about?'

'Nothing in particular. I remember that the major was anxious to leave as soon as he could. Something about re-joining his regiment, I believe. He said he had wasted far too much time already. Doctor Hollinger was urging restraint, saying it would look bad if you returned, Inspector, and found that he had left so suddenly,' said Jenkins, replacing his spectacles.

'I see. How were the major and Dr Hollinger?'

'I'm sorry, Inspector. I don't quite understand.'

'How did they seem? Were they arguing? Were sharp words exchanged between the two men?'

'I don't believe so. The major may have raised his voice once or twice, but nothing untoward. They were just sitting drinking amicably together when I left. Of course, they might have had words together afterwards, but if they did, it was unknown to me.'

'Thank you, Mr Jenkins. I'm afraid I am going to insist that you all remain here while we make attempts to discover the whereabouts of the major,' said Ravenscroft knowing that his words would be unpopular.

'For goodness sake, you can see how distressed Miss Eames is. I think it would be better if we three left as soon as possible. You know where we reside, if you need to contact us again once you have caught Major Anstruther,' said Ganniford, growing red in the face.

'I think the inspector would prefer us to remain,' interjected Jenkins, seeking to calm his friend.

'We must do all we can, Nathaniel, to bring the murderer to account,' added Miss Eames.

'Thank you,' said a relieved Ravenscroft.

'Then there is this Ross fellow. You don't have him either. Seems to me as though Ross and Anstruther were probably in it together,' offered Ganniford.

'Oh, why do you say that?' asked Ravenscroft.

'Well, it stands to sense. Ross disappeared once we were in the abbey. Probably came back here last night to meet up with the major, so that they could kill Hollinger together.'

'And why would they do that?'

'I don't know, do I? You are the detective,' replied an annoyed Ganniford.

'It would have nothing to do with a gold goblet, would it?'

A long silence followed as Ravenscroft noted the unease that his words had caused on his three suspects.

'I see, Inspector, that you have had words with Mr Ross,' said Jenkins eventually breaking the silence.

'Indeed. I now know the real reason for your visit,' continued Ravenscroft, anxious to follow up his advantage.

'We did not believe a word of it, of course,' said Jenkins. 'It was clear to all of us that the man was some kind of fraudster.'

'And yet, you all decided to come.'

'Curiosity, my dear Inspector. We were all curious to see how things would proceed. Is that not so, Ganniford?' asked Jenkins.

'Yes. Yes, certainly. Knew the man was a crook. That was it,' muttered an embarrassed Ganniford.

'And you, Miss Eames? Did you believe that there was a golden goblet waiting to be discovered?' asked Ravenscroft.

'I concur with what Mr Jenkins has just said,' replied the lady.

'So none of you came here in anticipation of gaining riches?'

Another silence followed as Ravenscroft's question remained unanswered.

'If you will all excuse me, I must make further enquiries regarding Major Anstruther, and to see whether we can locate the said gentleman as soon as possible.'

* * *

'Sit down if you will. We will not detain you long,' said Ravenscroft.

'Be glad when all this is over,' muttered the landlord of the Hop Pole looking visibly shaken as he accepted the seat.

'I am sorry for all the inconvenience, but, as you know, one of your guests has been killed in a most brutal fashion, and we have a duty to make inquiries.'

'Suppose so.'

'Another of your guests has also gone missing. Major Anstruther is not in his room this morning. Were you aware that the gentleman had left?'

'Paid his bill last night, he did,' replied the man shrugging his shoulders.

'I see,' said Ravenscroft looking across at Crabb. 'So the major said that he was leaving.'

'That's what I said.'

'What time was that?'

'About twelve.'

'Did the major take any luggage with him?' asked Crabb.

'He had a brown holdall. That's all.'

'How did he seem?' continued Ravenscroft, anxious to know more about his chief suspect's hasty departure.

'Don't know what you mean.'

'How did he seem to you? Did he seem anxious, or nervous in any way, as though he was in a hurry?'

'He seemed calm enough.'

'Did you notice anything unusual about his clothes? Was there any blood on them?'

'No. There was nothing unusual. He was wearing a big overcoat over his clothes. Couldn't see any blood. He just wanted to pay and leave. That's all I can tell you.'

'I see.'

'There was something he said though.'

'Go on,' said Ravenscroft leaning forwards across the table.

'He said he had to return to London as soon as possible. Something about his regiment was about to go off to India, and he had to be there.'

'And?'

'I told him that he had probably missed the last train out of Tewkesbury for London, and he would best wait for the early morning one.'

'What did he say to that?'

'Said it was no matter. He would find another way to get there.'

'That is interesting. Did he say how?'

'No. He just paid and left.'

'Thank you. You are certain it was around twelve when the major departed?'

'I remember the clock striking in the corner. There was one other thing.'

'Yes?' encouraged Ravenscroft.

'Well, when he left, he met someone outside. I saw them talking together.'

'Did you happen to see who it was?'

'The reverend.'

'You mean The Reverend Jesterson?'

'That's right.'

'What happened next?'

'After they had exchanged a few words, they went off together down the road.'

'You are absolutely sure it was The Reverend Jesterson you saw talking with the major? It must have been quite dark.'

'It is quite well lit out there. I'm sure it was Jesterson.'

'I see. Thank you, that is most informative. Oh, one more thing — when was the last time you saw Dr Hollinger?'

'About half past eleven. I noticed that both he and the major had been talking together in the snug. The doctor went upstairs first.'

'Leaving the major down here?'

'Yes.'

'What happened next?'

'The major went up a few minutes later.'

'Can you tell me how long elapsed between the major going upstairs and when he returned?'

'About fifteen minutes I should say.'

'You are sure on that point? Could it have been more or less than that?'

'No, it was fifteen minutes. I'm sure of it.'

'Thank you. You have been most helpful to us.'

'When can I have my room back?' asked the landlord, rising to his feet.

'I do not see why you should not reclaim the room now. The body has been taken to the mortuary, along with the sheets and the rest of Hollinger's effects.'

'I'd best clean it up then. Folks won't want to stay there once they knows what happened to the last gent that was in there,' said the man gloomily, as he left the room.

'Well, Tom, what do you make of that?' asked Ravenscroft.

'Seems like Anstruther had plenty of time to kill Hollinger,' replied Crabb.

'Yes, fifteen minutes would have been enough to slip into Hollinger's room, kill the doctor, wash his hands in the basin there, then return to his own room, discard the blood-stained clothes, pack and dress.'

'He was obviously anxious to get away as soon as possible.'

'That would make sense. If you or I had killed someone, we would have wanted to have quit the scene as quickly as possible, and to have put as much distance between ourselves and the body. Two things puzzle me, however. According to the landlord, Hollinger had retired only a few minutes before the major went upstairs. Would that have been long enough for him to have changed, got into his bed and fallen asleep before Anstruther entered the room?'

'Perhaps he fell asleep straight away,' suggested Crabb.

'That may have been so — but Anstruther would not have known that. Surely if he entered the doctor's room within a few minutes of his retiring, he would have run the risk of Hollinger still being awake. Surely it would have been more sensible to have waited for an hour or so?'

'He could have come back later?'

'Yes, there is that possibility. By leaving at twelve it would appear that he had already left the town by the time the murder was committed. I suppose he could have returned in the middle of the night, and slipped in and out unnoticed.'

'What about Jesterson, sir?' enquired Crabb.

'Yes, that is most interesting. I wonder if it was a chance encounter, or whether the two men had arranged to meet.'

'You think that Jesterson could be involved in Hollinger's murder?'

'At first sight it would seem unlikely. If Jesterson was involved, he surely would not have waited so conspicuously outside the Hop Pole for Anstruther to join him. No, I think our clergyman is of a too nervous disposition to be a party to this affair.'

'He seemed to know all about the inscription on the outside of the tomb. He could have been working on the solution for years.'

'You think his desire to unravel the code would have led him to participate in murder? I do not think so. He does not strike me as the type.'

'You said there was something else puzzling you,' asked a curious Crabb.

'Yes. If Anstruther did kill Hollinger just before twelve, why would he leave straight after? He must have known that the last train for London would have left earlier in the evening. Why not wait a few hours until nearly daylight, then he could have caught the first train out of the town.'

'There was always the chance that someone could have discovered Hollinger's body before then.'

'Highly unlikely, I would say.'

'What now?'

'We must try and find out what happened to Anstruther when he left here. We know he spoke to Jesterson. What happened next? Did they go off together? We know that Anstruther could not have caught the late train, as that had departed earlier in the evening, so where else could they have gone?'

'Perhaps he caught the early train out this morning?' suggested Crabb.

'We need to check at the station and see if the staff there saw anyone of his description. If he took the morning train to London, he could be anywhere by now and we may have little chance of apprehending him.'

'We could send a telegram to his regimental headquarters, sir.'

'We could, but I fear we may be wasting our time. If he is our killer, he would almost certainly know that would be the first place we would go looking for him. You may recall that your research showed that he probably wasn't who he claimed to be.'

'I noticed an old stables just up the road, sir. Maybe he went there and took one of the horses.'

'Good thinking, Tom. That seems more likely. I can't see the major waiting on a cold station platform all night. If that is the case, he won't have gone far. We will put out a description and telegraph it through to local stations.'

'Right, sir.'

'But first we need to have words with the reverend. And when we have done all that, I fancy we should return to Bredon's Norton and see if our mysterious Mr Ross has returned yet. There are some more questions I would like to put to him. We cannot rule out the possibility that he might have returned to Tewkesbury last night and killed Hollinger,' said Ravenscroft, pushing open the door of the snug and quickly making his way out onto the street.

* * *

A few minutes later, Ravenscroft and Crabb entered the abbey and made their way up the aisle to where a familiar figure could be seen near the altar.

'Good morning, gentlemen,' said Jesterson, looking up from his Prayer Book.

'Good morning, Reverend,' replied Ravenscroft. 'I wonder if I might have a few moments of your time?'

'Certainly, Inspector. I do hope that you have been able to catch the perpetrator of this terrible deed.'

'You mean Dr Hollinger, sir?'

'Doctor Hollinger? I'm sorry. I thought you were referring to the man in the tomb,' replied the bewildered clergyman.

'Of course, sir,' smiled Ravenscroft. 'I wonder if you could tell me what you were doing yesterday evening?'

'I'm sorry, I don't understand.'

'If you could just answer the question, sir, I would be obliged.'

'Well, Inspector, if you insist. I was at the abbey here until seven, then I went home as normal and spent the evening there.'

'What time did you retire, sir?'

'About half past twelve.'

'You did not go out before then, Reverend?' asked Crabb.

'No, I don't think so. Oh, yes! Yes, of course. I went out for a walk at around half past eleven.'

'Rather a late hour to be out walking?' asked Ravenscroft, his curiosity aroused.

'I must confess that I don't usually go out at such a late hour. I had retired to bed at around ten o'clock, but I could not sleep. I kept thinking of that poor man inside that tomb. Every time I opened my eyes I could see his face! What a dreadful, awful business! Who could have done such an unchristian thing?'

'So you went out for a walk,' said Ravenscroft.

'Yes, I thought that if I went out for a walk it would help to clear my mind.'

'What time did you return home?'

'I don't really remember. I must have been walking for at least an hour, I suppose,' replied Jesterson, nervously.

'Tell me, did you happen to meet anyone on your travels?'

'I don't believe so. There were not many people about in the town at that time of night, as I am sure you will understand.'

'So you spoke to no one?'

'No, I don't think so.'

'Outside the Hop Pole?' suggested Ravenscoft.

'The Hop Pole?'

'The landlord of the Hop Pole remembers you speaking to Major Anstruther outside the Hop Pole just after twelve o'clock.'

'Oh yes, of course. There was a military gentleman. He was just coming away from the Hop Pole. How silly of me not to have remembered.'

'What did Major Anstruther say to you?' asked Ravenscroft, after giving Crabb a knowing glance.

'He asked me if I knew of any stables in the town where he could acquire a horse. I told him that there was one further down the road, but I doubted that it would be open at such a late hour.'

'What happened next?'

'He thanked me for my answer then he walked away.'

'That is most interesting, sir, because the landlord of the Hop Pole distinctly recalls that the two of you walked away together from the inn.'

'Well, yes, I suppose we must have walked a few yards down the road, before we each went our separate ways. I remember we walked as far as the corner, then I returned home, leaving the gentleman to find his own way to the stables. Yes that is what happened.'

'Thank you, Reverend, you have been most helpful. One more thing, can I ask you whether you visited the Hop Pole at all last night?'

'No. What a curious question. Why should I have gone there?'

'Then I can take it that you did not?'

The clergyman nodded.

'Thank you again,' said Ravenscroft walking away.

'You will let me know when you have caught the terrible person who killed that poor man?'

'Of course. You will be kept fully informed.'

'You think he was telling us the truth, sir? He seemed very nervous, as though he had something to hide,' said Crabb, as the two men walked away from the abbey.

'I have no reason to doubt him. At least we now know that Anstruther was looking for a horse to effect his departure from the town.'

Later that afternoon Ravenscroft and Crabb stood in the empty room of Ross's house in the village of Bredon's Norton. Outside, the sun, which had made a brief appearance in the sky, had as yet failed to penetrate the gloom of the interior.

'He is nowhere to be seen, sir,' said a bewildered Crabb.

'It is as if no one has lived here for years. Even the fire looks as though it has not been lit this morning. There is nothing of a personal nature here, Tom — no clothes, no food or wine on the table, no portraits on the walls. It is almost as though we have come to another house. The only thing which appears to be the same is the intense coldness and misery of the place.'

'Perhaps our friend Ross does not live here at all,' suggested Crabb. 'He could have just been staying here.'

'Listen, Tom, do you hear that noise,' interrupted Ravenscroft.

'It sounds like a dog barking, somewhere in the distance.'

The two men walked quickly away from the room, closing the door of the house behind them.

'Over there!' said Ravenscroft pointing. 'Quickly, Crabb, stop that fellow and ask him to join us if you will.'

Crabb ran across the grass and returned a moment later with an old, bearded man wearing a long torn overcoat. A black and white sheepdog followed at his heels.

'I wonder if we might have a moment of your time, sir,' began Ravenscroft.

'Depends on whose asking,' replied the man.

'Inspector Ravenscroft of the Ledbury Constabulary, and this is my colleague Constable Crabb.'

'Ledbury you say. You be a long way from Ledders.'

'We are making investigations into a crime that has been committed in Tewkesbury. Can you tell me whether you reside locally?'

'Live at farm down road,' said the old man patting the head of his dog.

'Have you been there long?'

'Eighty years, man and boy.'

'Then you can tell me who lives in the house over there.'

'No one at present. House been empty for past ten years.'

'We were given to understand that a Mr Charles Ross resides there,' said Ravenscroft, hoping that the farmer might be able to offer a solution to the mystery.

'Ross you say. He used to live there. He weren't 'ere for long though.'

'Can you describe this Mr Ross for us?'

The man stared at Ravenscroft in silence.

'It is very important that we find Mr Ross and speak to him. Can you confirm our description — tall, thin man, approximately thirty in years, black hair, staring eyes, very bad cough.'

'That be him. Spoke in a funny way.'

'He has a Scottish accent,' added Crabb.

'Could be,' replied the man turning away and looking down at his dog. 'Come on now, Red, time for yer supper.'

'One more thing, just before you go — when did you last see Mr Ross?' asked Ravenscroft.

'About ten year ago.'

'Ten years ago!' exclaimed a frustrated Ravenscroft. 'You have not seen him for ten years?'

'That's what I said,' said the farmer beginning to take his leave.

'I find that difficult to believe. I spoke to Mr Ross only yesterday, in this same house.'

'Impossible. You must be mistaken,' called out the old man.

'We were both here, my constable and myself, and spoke to Mr Ross. Why do you say it was impossible?' asked a perplexed Ravenscroft.

'Because Mr Ross is dead. That's why. He were shot in a hunting accident ten years ago!'

CHAPTER SIX

LEDBURY AND OXFORD

Ravenscroft took out his pocket watch, noted that the time was two hours past midnight, and reached out to stir the dying embers in the hearth before him. A solitary candle on the table at his side cast flickering shadows on the walls of the house, as he bought the remains of the glass to his lips.

His thoughts turned once more to the empty house at Bredon's Norton, and he saw again the cold, inhospitable room and its strange occupant. The old man had been quite adamant that Ross had died ten years earlier as the result of a hunting accident when his firearm had blown up in his face — an assertion which had been confirmed by at least two other people with long memories who resided in the area — and yet that could not have been the case, as he and Crabb had spoken with the Scotsman earlier that day. Then there was the entry in the directory stating that a Mr Charles Ross was still resident at the house — and his three remaining suspects had all said that Ross had been there with them that night at the abbey. No, the old man and his neighbours must have been wrong. Ross was certainly very much alive, and had not been killed as the result of some shooting accident.

The man must have been thinking of someone else who had come to an untimely demise. Perhaps Ross had once lived in the house, and had left the area many years previously and had recently returned, unnoticed by his neighbours, only to disappear now once more into the unknown. But then if he had returned, why had he done so? The others had certainly confirmed the missing goblet story, so that had probably been the reason for his return, and yet if he had not been resident in the house when he had first been approached by the deceased stranger Crosbie, where had he been? Perhaps he had been in league with the man, planning the whole enterprise together — but if that had been the case, how did it explain the brutal stabbing of Hollinger?

Then there was Anstruther. What part had he played in all this? His discussion with the doctor before they had both retired for the night, the bloodstained clothes left behind in his bedroom, and his sudden midnight departure from the Hop Pole, all these facts seemed to implicate him in the killing. Crabb's inquiries at the stable yard further up the road, had confirmed what Jesterson had said, revealing that one of the horses had been taken in the night, so it appeared more than likely that the major had left the town in a hurry. Everything seemed to point to his guilt. A telegram sent to his regimental headquarters had confirmed what he and Crabb had suspected, namely that Anstruther had never been a member of the Guards. Clearly the man had set out to deceive everyone by exaggerating his own importance, and now had gone to ground. But why had Anstruther killed Hollinger — what possible reason could he have had to want to murder the poor man? Maybe Anstruther had been in league with the deceased Crosbie, in which case Ross was innocent. But if Ross had killed neither Crosbie nor Hollinger, why had he now gone to ground? The whole thing did not make sense — unless of course, Anstruther, Ross and Crosbie had all been in it together.

Why had either Anstruther or Ross, or both of them, killed Hollinger? What kind of threat had the Prussian doctor posed to them? Had he stood in the way of them finding the golden goblet? All his suspects had stated that they had not believed a word that had been told to them by the deceased Crosbie, and yet they had all chosen to keep the appointment outside the abbey; six complete strangers — except for the friends Jenkins and Ganniford — meeting for the first time, all said to be descendants of the crusader knight Sir Roger de la Pole, and all hoping to recover the ancient golden goblet. Had they found that treasure inside the tomb that night, or had Crosbie lifted it out of the grave earlier that same evening, handing it to his accomplice who then killed him in such brutal fashion? But if the goblet had been found, why had the killer then chosen to remain in the town instead of escaping as quickly as possible with his treasure? Perhaps the whole goblet story was pure fantasy. There had never been such a treasure in the first place, and Sir Roger had gone to his grave leaving no secrets behind him.

Then there was the greatest mystery of all. If there had been a treasure waiting to be discovered, why had not Crosbie just taken it for himself? Why had he chosen to involve the six strangers? Why had he visited them each in turn, using a different name each time, acquired from the novels of Anthony Trollope, informing them they were all descended from the Templar Knight, and urging them towards the fatal meeting?

No, the whole thing made no sense at all, and no matter how many times he considered the evidence, examining it from all the possible angles, every solution he came up with seemed to contradict one another.

'Samuel, do come to bed.'

The voice startled him, breaking into his deliberations and returning him abruptly to the present.

'It is nearly three o'clock in the morning,' said Lucy, kneeling before him and looking up into his face. 'You will be very tired in the morning, Samuel.'

'I am sorry, my dear. I keep going over and over this case in my mind. But no matter from which way I look at it, none of it makes the slightest sense,' said Ravenscroft, taking his wife's hands in his own.

'Perhaps in the morning you will see things in a different light.'

'I do not think so. I do believe this is the most difficult case I have ever undertaken in the whole of my career. I can see no reason why any of the parties involved would have committed these crimes. Not only do I have two dead bodies on my hands, but also two missing suspects.'

'Perhaps Tom will track one of them down tomorrow, or you may gain new inspiration in the morning,' suggested Lucy.

'Dear Lucy, you are my only source of inspiration,' smiled Ravenscroft, looking deeply into his wife's eyes. 'I do not know how I managed all those years without you. But I have been entirely selfish. I have been most neglectful in my duties as a husband.'

'Give me your hand,' said Lucy reaching out.

Ravenscroft rose from his chair and, taking his wife's hand, moved across to the window. 'I promise you that once this case is over, we will take the very next train to London. We are both in need of some entertainment and a change of scenery.'

'I shall keep you to that, Samuel Ravenscroft,' smiled Lucy.

'Look there in the sky, my dear. Do you see that star? Just there to our left. See how brightly it shines in the clear moonlit sky,' said Ravenscroft, drawing his wife closer to him, and placing his arms around her waist. 'One would think that it is the only star in the heavens tonight, and yet we know that there are many more in the universe. Sometimes, when I was in Whitechapel and the air was oppressive and I could not sleep at night, I would travel out to the heath at Hampstead and climb the hill there so that I could look down on the great city. There I would gradually clear my mind of all the crime and unpleasantness that lay beneath me, and remind myself of all the goodness and honesty that often lies hidden in the world. Then I would wonder whether I would ever leave that place, the bustling, noisy, smoke-ridden city, and what the future would hold for me. All that seems such a long time ago now. I little dreamt then that my life would so suddenly change for the better. That was only a year ago. And now I have you, my love, and you have given me a new purpose to my life. It often seems that I have been here in Ledbury, with you, for years. So you see, one must always have hope that things will become better, and that one's lot will be improved. I wonder who else tonight is looking upwards at that same star? Let you and I, my dear Lucy, adopt that star. Let it become our talisman, the source of all our hope and expectation. We must not despair. We must go forward.'

'You are quite the romantic, Samuel Ravenscroft,' said Lucy leaning her head on her husband's shoulder.

'I will find out who killed that poor man in the tomb and Dr Hollinger. We must have courage to go on. All will be well, of that I am sure. Now, I think it is time that we both sought out the comfort of our bed. Tomorrow will shortly be upon us, and we will both need our sleep if we are to gain inspiration from the new dawn.'

Lucy said nothing as she kissed her husband's cheek.

'Come, my dear.'

'I have been thinking of your case all night,' began Lucy, as they started to climb the stairs.

'I am sure that you have, but no more. Let us forget the whole thing for a few hours.'

'Perhaps the answer lies with your Sir Roger de la Pole, or whatever his name was.'

'Oh, why do you say that?'

'Well, he is, after all, the reason why your six suspects and the deceased man came to Tewkesbury. Perhaps if you were to turn your attention more to him than your five suspects, and try to find out more about him, then you might be able to discover what all this is about.'

'My dear Lucy, yes of course!' exclaimed Ravenscroft. 'In all this conjecture, I have been forgetting the most obvious course of action. You have pointed me in the right direction. Am I not married to a genius?'

'There, I told you that you would find inspiration. How will you find out more concerning your Sir Roger?'

'There are no doubt a number of books in the local library, and the clergyman at the abbey may be able to throw some more light on our old Templar. Of course, Professor Salt! Why did I not think of him before? Yes, I know a man who I can consult; Mathias Salt.'

'Mathias Salt?'

'Mathias Tobias Salt, Professor of Medieval Studies, to give him his full title.'

'And where does this Professor Salt reside?' enquired Lucy opening the door to their bedroom.

'In one of the darker corners of Oxford, hidden away from all view, and no doubt engaged on some great historical research. I remember that I had reason to consult him many years ago, when he was able to assist me in the solving of a very difficult case. Yes, I shall take the early morning train for Oxford. Tom can carry on the search for Ross and Anstruther. Salt may well have the answers to all this.'

* * *

Ravenscroft stared up at the imposing ancient building which cast long deep shadows on the neatly cut lawns before him. The journey by train to Oxford had been uneventful and he had enjoyed the pleasant walk along the busy streets of the town before entering the grounds of the college.

'Careful, my dear sir!' exclaimed a young man running into the quadrangle and colliding with Ravenscroft.

'I am so sorry,' began Ravenscroft. 'I should have been paying more attention. I was admiring the architecture of your college.'

'Not bad, is it?' said the young man picking up a pile of papers which had dropped to the ground.

'You are most fortunate to be a student here. Would that I had been granted the same opportunity in my youth.'

'It's not all that people would have you believe, you know. The rooms are freezing cold in winter, the food is barely passable, company is of a mediocre quality, and a great deal of the tuition leaves a lot to be desired. Anyway, can't stop now. No time to talk. An interesting lecture on eighteenth century politics in the Sheldonian beckons.'

'Could you tell me where I might find the residence of Professor Salt?' asked Ravenscroft.

'Over there, up two flights of stairs, knock on number sixteen.' came back the hasty reply as the young man ran off at a brisk pace.

'Thank you.'

Ravenscroft entered the building and began to make his way up the worn stone steps.

After a few moments, he reached the second-storey landing and made his way along the corridor, reading the numbers on the oak doors until he reached one that bore the number sixteen. Raising his hand he tapped gently on the woodwork and listened for any sound from within the ancient room. Receiving no reply he repeated the action in a louder fashion.

'Come in,' bellowed a voice, somewhere in the distance.

Ravenscroft opened the door and entered the room. An old, tall, grey-haired, bearded man was seated at a large desk in the centre, busily engaged in examining what Ravenscroft supposed to be some kind of ancient document.

Ravenscroft coughed.

'What did you say your name was, my dear boy?' asked the voice without looking up at the new arrival.

'I didn't. But my name is Ravenscroft.'

'Ravenscroft?'

'Detective Inspector Ravenscroft.'

'Ravenscroft? I have certainly heard that name somewhere before. You look familiar. Have we met sometime in the distant past?' said the questioner casting a brief glance in his direction before resuming his studies.

'About ten years ago. I had need to consult you regarding the demise of Sir Charles Foulsome,' offered Ravenscroft, hoping that the old man would recall their earlier meeting.

'Foulsome, you say. I can't say I recall the name.'

'You were kind enough to translate an old will for me, which, as it proved, had a distinct bearing on the case,'

'Ah yes, I do remember! Case of a forged signature and all that, and some dubious legacies if I recall. Ravenscourt, you said?'

'Ravenscroft,' said the detective, shaking the hand that had suddenly been offered.

'And how can I be of assistance to you, Inspector?'

'I wonder if you could tell me anything about the Knights Templar and about one of their number in particular, namely Sir Roger de la Pole of Tewkesbury,' asked Ravenscroft, relieved that he had at last obtained the learned man's attention.

'Ah, the Templars! Interesting group of people. To give them their full title, Knights Templar or Order of Poor Knights of Christ and the Temple of Solomon — although many of them were far from poor. They were a kind of religious military order, formed around 1119, with the purpose of protecting pilgrims as they travelled to the Holy Land. They played an important role in the crusades. Pope Innocent II even placed them under direct papal authority.'

'You say that many of them became quite wealthy. Why was this?'

'As the various crusader states declined in authority, they increasingly found themselves in the role of financiers and bankers of the crusading enterprise. People often forget that many of the crusades might not have taken place at all were it not for the money provided by the Templars. Religious endeavour is all very well, but it is money that pays for food and weapons. Such a state of affairs could not continue for long of course. Philip IV of France and the Avignon Pope Clement V decided to suppress the order, claiming that they had become heretics, but really resenting the independence, power and wealth of the brotherhood. Money can often lead to corruption, Inspector, and even if it does not, jealousy can be a dangerous thing to countenance,' continued Professor Salt, stroking his long white beard and staring at Ravenscroft through the lenses of his narrow-framed spectacles.

'What happened to the Templars?' asked Ravenscroft becoming more interested in the subject.

'Many of them were rounded up by the authorities and put to death, but some did escape persecution. A number of them joined the order of the Knights of St John and fought against the Turks on the islands of Rhodes and Malta. Some, no doubt, returned home, like your Sir Roger de la Pole, where they were fortunate enough to die in their own beds.'

'And the order?'

'Completely extinguished, although some say that there are descendants who are intent on continuing with the order, in secret, to this day, though I hasten to say that if there are any remaining Templars I certainly have never come across them.'

'What can you tell me about Sir Roger?'

'Ah, a most interesting family, the de la Poles. The first one to achieve prominence was William de la Pole, a rich merchant and ship owner who helped to finance Edward III in his campaign against the French. A very shrewd business man by all accounts. Then there was Michael de la Pole, financier and royal servant who became chancellor to Richard II, before being forced to flee to France to escape impeachment on charges of embezzlement and negligence. Very careless to say the least. After him there was his grandson, William de la Pole, who fought with Henry V at Agincourt no less, but who fared less well under his son Henry VI, where he was sent to the Tower on charges of treason and corruption. He came to a rather bloody end, beheaded by a group of dissidents as he tried to escape the country. Edmund de la Pole seems not to have fared any better, being executed by Henry VIII. They seem to have been rather intent in making a habit of annoying royalty and paying the ultimate price.'

'And Sir Roger de la Pole?' interrupted Ravenscroft, anxious to turn the conversation back to the Templar Knight.

'Came from another, poorer and less illustrious branch of the family, I believe, who saw the prudence of keeping well in the background, thus avoiding any controversy and thereby managing to keep their heads.'

'You seem remarkably well informed about the de la Poles,' said Ravenscroft.

'Medieval history is my speciality, my dear boy, although you must have known that, or you would not have made the journey to visit me today,' replied the professor moving his glasses further down his elongated nose so that he was able to stare at his questioner above their lens.

'Of course,' said Ravenscroft quickly, anxious not to cause offence. 'And would Sir Roger have returned from the Holy Land with any kind of treasure?'

'Ah, I see where this is going! You believe that Sir Roger returned bearing gold, frankincense and all kinds of precious goods.'

'There was talk of a golden goblet,' offered Ravenscoft.

'Not in any documents of the time, as I recall.'

'So it would have been unlikely?'

'Unlikely, but not impossible. Just because it was not recorded at the time, does not lead one to the conclusion that there was no such treasure. If Sir Roger was able to acquire something of value on his travels, or in Jerusalem, then he would probably have kept very quiet about it.'

'If there had been such a golden goblet, said to be encrusted with precious jewels, what do you think it could possibly have been?'

'Ah, I see thoughts of the Holy Grail are entering your mind!' exclaimed Salt lifting his hands above his head and clapping them together.

'I'm sorry, I don't understand,' said Ravenscroft, somewhat taken aback by the suddenness of the learned man's strange behaviour.

'All through history there have been strange fantasies concerning the Holy Grail, the cup or goblet which our Christ used at the Last Supper and which was said to contain His very own blood collected from His body at the Crucifixion. Nonsense, all of it! If such a cup, goblet or container had been used, let alone preserved, then it would almost certainly have been made of wood, or some other form of perishable material. Gold encrusted goblets indeed! A nonsensical idea carried forward through the centuries, later to be embellished by those stories made up about that vagabond King Arthur and his so-called Knights of the Round Table and their search for the Holy Grail. Nonsense — dangerous nonsense all of it,' continued the professor becoming more animated during his discourse.

'I see, then there would have been no golden goblet bought home by Sir Roger?'

'Forget all this Grail nonsense. If Sir Roger did return with some keepsake or artefact, it would not have been a golden goblet I am sure.'

'Do you think that if Sir Roger did return with something of value, it could have been placed in his tomb when he died?' asked Ravenscroft.

'Highly unlikely I would say. You would run the risk that someone would have helped themselves to the item either when he was entombed, or that someone would have returned within a few days to force open the tomb and appropriate it for themselves. More likely he passed it on to another member of his family before his death.'

'Do you think he could have hidden it somewhere?'

'Why do you ask that?'

'We found some rather strange marks on the outside of Sir Roger's tomb.'

'Do you have a record of such markings?' enquired the professor, his curiosity aroused.

'My constable jotted them down in his notebook,' said Ravenscroft, producing the item from his own pocket and handing it to the professor.

'Most interesting,' said the scholar readjusting his spectacles and bringing the book closer towards his eyes.

CR4 * Q1 * BR3 * CR4 *Q1 * Q2 BL2 * KL2 * +3 * CL2 * Q2 * CR1 * CL1

'No one seems to know what it means.'

'I can see why that has been the case. At first sight it looks quite perplexing,' said Salt, twitching his nose so alarmingly that Ravenscroft thought the scholar might be in imminent danger of losing his spectacles. 'I think that you had perhaps better inform me as to the nature of your case, my dear boy.'

During the next few minutes Ravenscroft narrated in some detail all the facts concerning the dead man found inside the crusader's tomb and all that had followed on from his investigation, ending with the disappearance of Ross and the flight of Anstruther, during which the professor paced up and down in deep thought, pausing now and then to exclaim such phrases as 'well I never' and 'how extraordinary'.

'And there you have it,' said Ravenscroft coming to the end of his discourse.

'Well, well. An interesting state of affairs. I can appreciate your difficulties, my dear Inspector. Difficulties indeed. I must say that I am inclined to agree with your premise that your six suspects all decided to keep their appointment at the abbey in the expectation of discovering Sir Roger's treasure. If we assume that the goblet, or whatever we like to call it, was not buried with Sir Roger, then it must be somewhere else, and that is where your strange markings come to the fore.'

'I was hoping that you might be able to decipher the letters.'

Ravenscroft watched as the antiquary first bought the paper close to his face where he peered at the letters and numbers for some moments, before closing his eyes and clasping his forehead as if in pain.

'Why everyone who has sought to obtain meaning from these symbols has failed, is because they have tried to solve the problem from their own perspective and time,' pronounced the professor eventually, waving the paper in the air.

'Go on,' urged Ravenscroft, hoping that his words of encouragement might bear fruit.

'What we must do, if we are to solve this problem, is to look at it from Sir Roger's point of view; after all it was he, one presumes, who gave instruction for the message to be written on his tomb. Why did he do this? He wanted to make sure that only someone of sufficient intelligence, of a similar background and experience as himself, who came after him, would be able to work out what the message means. Sir Roger was clearly a man who enjoyed a good sense of humour. I rather like him, I must say!'

Ravenscroft smiled, but wondered whether all the professor's deliberations would eventually lead to the solution he was hoping for.

'Sir Roger had recently returned from the Holy Land. Out there he would have encountered another world, where the sights, smells and sounds would have all been different — more important even the language, both written and spoken, would have been unusual. Arabic writing is read from the right. It proceeds across the page until it reaches the left-hand side.'

'So we have been reading the message the wrong way round!' exclaimed Ravenscroft.

'Exactly.'

'But it still does not make sense, even when you read it backwards.'

'Ah, that is where the second element of the puzzle begins. Chess!' announced the old man triumphantly. 'You play chess, Mr Ravenscroft?'

'Not for many years.'

'But you are no doubt aware of the rules. Chess is an ancient game, stretching back over two thousand years. When Sir Roger went on his crusade, chess was completely unknown in England, but in the Holy Land it was already established. Sir Roger must have seen the game and decided to work it into his little puzzle. By adopting both the Arabic way of writing and the game of chess, both of which would have been unknown to his contemporaries at home, he was ensuring that only someone like himself, a crusader knight, another Templar, would have been able to solve the clues and work out what the message says.'

'And would have been rewarded for his efforts,' added Ravenscroft.

'Exactly!'

'Like a gentleman's club?'

'A very select gentlemen's club, my dear Ravenscroft.'

'So do you think we could now solve the puzzle?'

'Ah well, that may be difficult — but not perhaps impossible. Here, take this large sheet of paper and this ruler — and with this pen draw a chessboard, eight squares across and eight the other way.'

Ravenscroft did as he was instructed, as the antiquary, stroking his flowing beard, continued to stare hard at the paper before him.

'Good. This will be our chessboard. Bearing in mind that Arabic script is written from right to left, I want you to place each letter of the alphabet, in order, in each square, commencing with the "a" in the bottom right-hand square and so on.'

Ravenscroft did as he was instructed, ending the first bottom row of the board with the letter 'h', the second row ending in 'p', the third with 'x'.

'There are two letters left over, "y" and "z" — where shall I place those?'

'In the first two squares of the next row,' replied the professor leaning over his shoulder. 'Good, now do the same with your opponent, starting again with the 'a' in the last right-hand square of the back row, and then moving leftwards across the board.'

'Surely one's opponent would have been facing the other way,' corrected Ravenscroft.

'True, but I believe that the board is meant to be seen by one person, namely the reader of the inscription and, as such, the letters would again run from right to left.'

Ravenscroft again wrote in all the letters on the paper.

'Excellent, my dear inspector. So we now have both the 'a's facing one another and so on. Now mark on the paper, outside the main board, the names of the pieces.'

Ravenscroft wrote 'castle' facing the square which bore the letter 'a' 'knight' facing the letter 'b' and so on, until he had completed the back row.

'Now do the same with your opponent's side of the board. Excellent. Now we are ready to begin. What we clearly have is two words, one written underneath the other. If we assume that white begins the game first, at the bottom of the board, then we can conclude that the first word on the inscription is played by white and that the second word, is played by black at the top of the board. Now remembering that the word is written from right to left, we look at the first group of letters and numbers, namely Q2—'

'Q stands for the queen,' interrupted Ravenscroft, fascinated by the learned man's conclusions.

'So, if the queen moves two squares forward, from the edge of the board, then we arrive at the letter M. Now if we take the next group Q1 and this time only move the queen forward one square from the edge of the board, which in fact is its starting position, we reveal the letter E. The next group poses a problem, CR4. Ah yes, I have it! C stands for the castle, and because there are two of them, the letter R suggests the castle to the right. Now move four squares to the front, departing from the edge of the board, and we arrive at the letter Y. Likewise, BR3 relates to the bishop on the right side, which when we move it forward gives us the letter S. Q1 gives us the letter E again, and CR4 will give us the letter Y. Now you try to decipher the second word, for your opponent, black, remembering to start from the right. I believe that the letter K represents the knight and that the "+ 3" probably stands for the king as he is the most important piece on the board.'

Intrigued, Ravenscroft worked through the second group of letters, revealing the word HAMPTON after a few minutes work. 'Meysey Hampton — what on earth does that mean?' he asked, finally laying down his pen and looking intently at the two words before him.

'It's a place, my dear Ravenscroft. A place. Wait here!' instructed the professor, rushing quickly out of the room, leaving a bewildered Ravenscroft behind him. The learned antiquary may well have deciphered the inscription on the side of the old crusader's tomb, revealing the two new words, thought Ravenscroft, but the whole thing did not appear to be any clearer to him.

'Ah, here we are,' said Salt, returning triumphantly to the room bearing a large thick volume which he flung down on the table, before intently running his finger along several lines of script on the open page. 'Here we have it! Meysey Hampton, ancient Gloucestershire parish, north of Cirencester, close to the market town of Fairford. Ah, ah! Now everything is revealed. The church of Meysey Hampton is said to have been built by the Templar Knights! It is a Templar church and that is why the inscription was placed on the side of Sir Roger's tomb.'

'But why? Why would Sir Roger have left instructions for such an elaborate code to be written on the side of his tomb?' asked Ravenscroft.

'Sir Roger knew that only another Templar would have been able to work out that the numbers and letters when placed on a chessboard, would reveal the name of Meysey Hampton. He was clearly sending a message that his fellow knights should go to the church in that village.'

'I see, so if there was any treasure to be found, it would be at this Meysey Hampton?'

'That is still a matter of conjecture. We do not know that Sir Roger bought anything of value back with him from his travels. He might have simply been referring to another church in Gloucestershire, with which he had some association, that is all,' replied Salt, smiling at Ravenscroft.

'So what do you think I should do now?' asked Ravenscroft, feeling as though he was addressing a benevolent uncle.

'That is for you to decide, I have merely unravelled the code.'

'For which I shall be forever in your debt, Professor Salt.'

'Say no more, my boy. I relish the challenge! But now if you will excuse me, I must return to my studies. I have to give a lecture in hall tomorrow night on manorial land management as seen through medieval Latin manuscripts,' said the professor turning away.

'There is just one more thing before I go. Do you think there are any living descendants of Sir Roger, and if so, how would we go about locating them?'

'With difficulty. Leave me your name and address on the way out and I will see if I can find out anything for you,' said Professor Salt, leaning over his ancient manuscript and already lost in another world.

Ravenscroft tore out a page from his notebook and, after writing his details, placed it on the table and made his way quietly from the room. The antiquary did not look up as he closed the door behind him.

As he walked through the town towards the railway station, Ravenscroft found himself turning over the events of the last half-hour, seeing again the elaborate code, the chessboard with its letters of the alphabet placed in each square and finally the revealing of the words 'Meysey Hampton'. Had the Templar Knight returned from his travels having appropriated something of great value? Had he then hidden that treasure somewhere in the remote Gloucestershire village of Meysey Hampton, instructing the stonemason who carved his tomb to engrave the mysterious letters on the side of the edifice, making the code so difficult that it would only make sense to another member of the same knightly order? Or did the revealed letters merely inform those fortunate enough to decipher them that Sir Roger had some connection with the Templar church in that village? Perhaps he should visit the church for himself and see if Sir Roger had left any further clues there, which might eventually lead to the discovery of the lost treasure. All this deciphering of medieval codes was all very well, Ravenscroft told himself, but although he was now in possession of facts that had not been discernible to others through the centuries, that gaining of knowledge seemed to be of little assistance to him in his quest to discover the truth behind the two murders he was intent on solving.

'Here, look out, mister, where you are going,' said a tall young man colliding with Ravenscroft.

'I am so sorry. My thoughts were elsewhere. Forgive me, my dear sir.'

'Should be more careful at your age,' grumbled the youth, picking up his papers which had fallen to the ground. 'I say haven't I seen you somewhere before?'

'You were kind enough to give me directions to Professor Mathias Salt's rooms.'

'Ay yes. I trust you were able to find the learned professor?'

'Yes, thank you. How was your lecture?'

'Disappointing to say the least. I should have foreseen that such would be the case. Should have remained in my rooms and read the book instead. But there you are. One lives in expectation and then one is constantly let down. That's life I suppose.'

'Indeed,' acknowledged Ravenscroft, smiling at the young man's philosophy.

'The trouble with these Oxford professors is that they think they are the only ones to offer a solution. They simply cannot comprehend that there are others out there who might be just as qualified to express a different point of view. Anyway, must go. No time to spare. Everything to be experienced. Nice meeting you.'

'And you, my good sir,' said Ravenscroft giving a brief smile, before taking his departure and continuing on his journey to the station.

Taking out his pocket watch and examining the noticeboard he was relieved to discover that a train was imminent.

Ravenscroft stood on the platform of the station, watching the billowing smoke of the approaching train, his mind still occupied by the events of the previous hour.

‘The trouble with these Oxford professors is that they think they are the only ones to offer a solution’ — that is what the young man had said. Then it suddenly occurred to Ravenscroft that perhaps after all there had been others who might have worked out what the strange letters and numbers had stood for on the side of the tomb. Professor Salt may not have been the only one. Perhaps Hollinger sitting in the snug of the Hop Pole that night had also been able to decipher the inscription. If that had been the case, then perhaps he had also written down the answer — and if that had been so, then that would explain why the learned doctor had been killed. Furthermore, if that is what transpired, then it was more than likely that his murderer was also now in possession of the solution.

CHAPTER SEVEN

TEWKESBURY

'We have him, sir!' exclaimed Crabb eagerly, as Ravenscroft alighted from the train.

'Anstruther?'

'At Hereford. Apparently he fell whilst endeavouring to change horses at one of the local inns. A doctor was called, and one of our men in the town thought that the stranger there might fit the description we had sent out earlier in the day.'

'Is he badly injured?'

'Broken arm by all accounts. I have instructed the men to bring him back to the station in Tewkesbury. He should be there by now, sir.'

'Good news, Tom. Well done.'

'How did you get on in Oxford?'

'Very well indeed. Professor Salt was able to decipher the inscription on Sir Roger's tomb, but more of that later. I am anxious to question the major. Let us see whether we can loosen his tongue. It is to be hoped that this mystery is now drawing to its conclusion. Lead on, Tom.'

* * *

'What the blazes is all this about, Ravenscroft?' said Anstruther, rising from the chair as the two policemen entered the room.

'I would have thought that was obvious, Major,' replied Ravenscroft, taking his seat behind the table and observing that his suspect had one of his arms in a sling and that his forehead was marked and bruised in several places.

'Not to me it's not,' snapped Anstruther. 'A fellow should be allowed to go where he wants to without being arrested by your heavy-handed peelers and forcibly bought back here against his will.'

'I am sorry for your injury. A horse, I believe. I trust it is not too painful,' said Ravenscroft forcing a brief smile.

'I've known worse.'

'I can arrange for another medical man to take a look at your arm, should you so wish.'

'Look here Ravenscroft, why the deuce have you bought me back here?'

'You are not aware that Dr Hollinger has been killed in a brutal fashion?' said Ravenscroft, staring straight at his suspect so that he could observe his reaction.

'What? Hollinger? Hollinger dead, you say?'

'Stabbed three times in the chest. Not a pleasant sight. But you would know that, of course.'

'What the blazes do you mean by that!' exclaimed Anstruther.

'Doctor Hollinger was murdered shortly after he retired last night. At twelve o'clock you were seen leaving the inn. I have two witnesses who can confirm your movements. Your bloodstained shirt and trousers were found in your room. How do you explain it?'

'Now look here, Ravenscroft, I don't know what you're talking about, but I know nothing about the doctor's death until you mentioned it now. As for my clothes, I took them all with me.'

'Your knife was found in the dead man's room.'

'I don't possess a knife,' protested Anstruther.

'I thought all army men carried a knife.'

'Well, you think wrong. I repeat, I do not possess any kind of knife.'

'So you deny having killed Dr Hollinger?'

'That's what I just said,' replied Anstruther, raising his voice.

'Then what were you doing leaving the Hop Pole at such a late hour?' asked Ravenscroft leaning back in his chair.

'Had enough of all this nonsense. I've got my regiment to return to. I couldn't afford to brook any further delay. Damn it, man, I've been here long enough!'

'I thought your regiment was based in London. You were arrested in Hereford after your fall. It is rather a long way round to get to the capital, is it not?'

'Had urgent business there,' mumbled Anstruther turning away.

'What business?'

'Private business. None of your concern.'

'I think this is all nonsense, Major Anstruther. If you were in such a great hurry to rejoin your regiment, as you claim, then surely you would have gone straight to London. I think you deliberately went in a westerly direction towards Hereford, rather than to the east, as you believed that we would be looking for you on the road to London. Is that not so?'

'I've told you, I had urgent business there,' retorted Anstruther growing red in the face as he stared at his inquisitor.

'Why did you leave at such a late hour? Surely you could have waited until the morning?' observed Ravenscroft, hoping that if he continued with his questioning, his suspect might eventually be forced to come forward with the truth.

'I was anxious to get on. I thought if I could get to Hereford by the morning I could conduct my business there, and then catch the London train later in the day.'

'You could have started earlier in the morning. Travelling by night along unknown country lanes can be quite difficult and dangerous, as I am sure you are aware.'

'We military men are used to that kind of thing. I knew that if I waited until the morning you would have prevented me from leaving. Damn it, Ravenscroft, you know as well as I do that it is important to do one's duty. Queen and country and all that. You're a man of the world; you understand these things. Wasted enough time around here over the past few days,' replied Anstruther, in a softer tone, hoping to placate his questioner.

'I think you killed Hollinger in his room, shortly after you both retired for the evening, you discarded your blood-stained clothes, and that you then left in a great hurry before the body was discovered.'

'That's not true. I've told you I took all my clothes with me. You can check if you so wish,' interrupted Anstruther.

'I don't think you are in the Guards at all. All this nonsense about doing one's duty,' continued Ravenscroft. 'In fact, I am damn certain that you have never been in the army in your life.'

'I've told you before, the directories are at fault. I can't help it if they have missed my name off the Army List.'

'My constable here sent a telegram to the Army Office yesterday. They have no record of a Major Anstruther serving in the army at present. It just won't do. Why don't you stop all this pretence about being in the Guards, and tell us the truth?' said Ravenscroft raising his voice.

'All right! All right, man! For goodness sake, stop going on,' retorted Anstruther slumping back in his chair.

'All we require is the truth. If you are not Major Anstruther then who are you?' said Ravenscroft pressing home his advantage.

'My name is John Anstruther. You are correct in your assumption. I have never been in the army. In fact I am an actor by profession.'

'An actor!' exclaimed Crabb looking up from his notebook.

'There's nothing dishonourable in being an actor,' replied Anstruther speaking in what Ravenscroft noticed to be a much quieter and relaxed tone of voice.

'Why did you pretend to be a major in the Guards?' asked Ravenscroft, anxious to know more.

'You know what people think of actors. I just thought I would play the part of an army major so that the others would look up to me. Be on more of an equal footing, if you see what I mean.'

'And the rest of it?'

'Oh, that's all true. The stranger, Grantly, that dead fellow in the tomb, came to my dressing-room after one of my appearances in London. Said I was a descendant of Sir Roger, and that I should agree to meet all the others outside the abbey, where we would all find where Sir Roger was buried and find a golden goblet he had bought back from the Holy Land.'

'Ah yes, the golden goblet,' smiled Ravenscroft.

'It was all nonsense, of course. I did not believe a word he said. The fellow clearly had a heightened imagination.'

'If you believed that to be the case, Mr Anstruther, why did you then decide to keep the appointment? Surely a man as busily engaged as yourself on theatrical performances would not have been free to spare the time on such a wanton errand?' asked Ravenscroft, leaning back in his chair once more.

'You're right, of course, Inspector. The truth of the matter is that he paid me.'

'Paid you, sir?' asked Crabb.

'Yes, he paid me ten guineas if I would leave off my run of the play for a few nights, and join the others in the abbey. That's why I was so anxious to get back to London. I have another performance tomorrow night,' said Anstruther, adopting a more flamboyant mode of speech.

'Oh, and what play would that be?' enquired Ravenscroft.

'*Richard III* at the Lyceum. I am playing Buckingham to the great Henry Irving's king. You can check there if you like.'

'We certainly will. Make a note, Crabb. All this is very well, Anstruther, but it changes nothing. What exactly were you and Hollinger talking about in the snug of the Hop Pole before you retired for the evening?'

'I can't remember.'

'I suggest that you try and remember. It might be important in your defence.'

'We just talked over the events of the last few days. Wondered when we would be free to leave. That sought of thing.'

'Did Dr Hollinger mention to you about the inscription?' asked Ravenscroft leaning forward again.

'What inscription?'

'Come now, Anstruther, you know perfectly well what I mean. The inscription on the side of Sir Roger's tomb.'

'I don't know what you mean,' replied the actor, a puzzled expression on his face.

'Oh I think you do. I think Hollinger told you that he had translated the inscription — and that is why you killed him, so that no one else would know where the treasure was hidden.'

'Look, this is all nonsense. I don't know what the blazes you are talking about. I had no reason to kill Hollinger.'

'And the bloodstained shirt and trousers?'

'I've told you, I took all my clothes with me.'

'And what exactly were you doing in Hereford?'

'I was visiting the theatre there. There may be a chance to play there sometime in the future. Look, now I have answered all your questions, surely you can see that all of this has been some kind of dreadful mistake. If you let me leave and return to London, I'll say no more about the rough way your officers have treated me,' said Anstruther, beginning to rise from his chair.

'I have to tell you, Mr Anstruther, that I am still not satisfied with your answers and that you remain the chief suspect in this affair. Crabb, escort Mr Anstruther back to his cell. Perhaps another night there might assist you in telling us the truth,' said Ravenscroft firmly.

'I've told you all I know. I have nothing to do with this murder. You must let me return to London. This is a scandal.'

'Crabb,' instructed Ravenscroft turning away.

'This way, sir, if you will,' said Crabb, placing a hand on the actor's arm.

'This won't do, Ravenscroft,' protested Anstruther brushing away the policeman's grip. 'I will summon my lawyer. I warn you, that you have not heard the last of this.'

A few minutes later Crabb returned to the room.

'Well, Tom, what do you make of all that?' asked Ravenscroft.

'Not much. Shifty characters these actors. Can't believe a word they say.'

'I must say I am inclined to agree with you, Tom. I don't feel that he was telling us the truth when he said he was appearing with the great Henry Irving at the Lyceum Theatre in London.'

'I'll send a telegram there right away.'

'Good, then we shall know whether he was telling us the truth, or whether he was just making up the story when we told him that he wasn't the army man he claimed to be. This story about being a famous actor may yet be another fabrication he was hoping we would swallow. One way or the other I am holding him in the cells until I get the truth from him. Do you think he killed Hollinger?' asked Ravenscroft, deep in thought.

'Looks that way sir — bloodstained clothes in his room, his hasty flight from the inn at midnight, the army knife. Then he was seen by both the landlord and Reverend Jesterson.'

'Yes it would seem that the man is guilty, but I am not entirely convinced. If you had killed a man in his bedroom why leave the knife behind, then change out of your bloodstained clothes and leave them behind in your own bedroom where they could easily be found? It seems rather a foolish thing to do. Far better to have taken them with you and dispose of them in a river somewhere.'

'Perhaps he wasn't thinking straight. Maybe in his panic to leave the town as quickly as possible, he just left them behind,' suggested Crabb.

'You could be right. If we assume that Hollinger had been successful in transcribing the inscription on the side of Sir Roger's tomb, and that he had either told Anstruther what the symbols stood for, or had written it down — and that Anstruther had then killed him to prevent him from telling the others that knowledge — why then did Anstruther decide to go in the opposite direction towards Wales? Surely he would have gone to Meysey Hampton instead?'

'Meysey what, sir?' asked a bewildered Crabb.

'Oh, I'm sorry, Tom. I meant to tell you that Professor Salt managed to solve the puzzle. The strange letters and numbers reveal the words Meysey Hampton. Apparently it's a village near the town of Fairford in Gloucestershire. It seems as though our Sir Roger may have had some association with the Templar church there.'

'I see — and you think that Anstruther should have gone there instead of Hereford?'

'One would have thought so, if he was after the treasure, unless of course he went deliberately in the other direction in order to distract us. To tell you the truth, I don't know what to think anymore. I do know, however, that I am sure that Mr Anstruther has a lot more to tell us. It is getting late. A night in the cells might persuade him to tell us more. We had better have a word with Miss Eames, Ganniford and Jenkins and insist that they spend another night here. We will also need to step up the search for that Ross fellow in the morning. Let us also send that telegram about Anstruther to the theatre in London — and we had better send out for some food for our prisoner before we return to our homes. We don't want Anstruther complaining that we have starved him to death.'

CHAPTER EIGHT

TEWKESBURY

As Crabb drove the trap round the winding lanes that lead from Ledbury to Tewkesbury, the following afternoon, Ravenscroft remained deep in thought, oblivious to his ever changing surroundings. Yesterday it had seemed that they had caught their killer — Anstruther, the bragging army major, who had confessed that he was really an actor by profession, had killed both the man in the tomb and Hollinger, so that he could acquire the treasure of the long deceased Templar for himself. It had all seemed so straightforward. But now Ravenscroft was not so sure. If Anstruther was the killer, why had he not travelled to Meysey Hampton as quickly as possible to seek out the treasure, instead of riding in the completely opposite direction? That would have been the obvious course of action to take. But if Anstruther was not the killer, why had he left the inn so suddenly? Why had he been in such a hurry? What secret was he hiding — and if he was not the killer, then who was?

'A penny for your thoughts, sir,' interjected Crabb.

'I keep thinking about the events of the last few days. Until that fellow Ross is found, I fear we will make little progress with the case.'

'There is still Anstruther, sir. We have him in custody.'

'Yes, perhaps a night in the cells will have loosened his tongue, and he might be more than inclined to tell us the truth today. We might have received a reply to our telegraph enquiry to the Lyceum in London. Let us hope we can solve the crime today; I don't think we can detain Miss Eames, Jenkins and Ganniford for much longer. I fear that Ganniford, in particular, will have his lawyers onto me if I insist he remains in Tewkesbury for another night.'

'You think that one of them might be our murderer?'

'In all honesty, I don't know. All I can say is that at present Ross and Anstruther seem our most likely candidates.'

* * *

As they drove into Tewkesbury, the sound of the church clock struck the hour of two. Ravenscroft alighted from the trap and made his way into the station.

'Good afternoon to you, sir,' said Constable Reynolds looking up from the large ledger spread out on the desk before him.

'Good afternoon to you, Reynolds,' replied Ravenscroft. 'How have things been here during our absence?'

'Not much to relate, sir. I've had Mr Ganniford round here this morning saying if they did not hear anything from you by later this afternoon, he and his party would be leaving on the five o'clock train. I told him that you would be back shortly and advised him against being too hasty. He wasn't too pleased, I can tell you.'

'No, I don't suppose he was, but that cannot be helped. How is our prisoner?' asked Ravenscroft as Crabb entered the room.

'Complaining all morning. Wanted to know why he had been left alone, and asking where you had gone to. He even threatened to have his lawyer onto us. I sent out for some more food for him about twelve, and since then I have not heard anything from him. Oh, and this telegram arrived for you, sir,' said Reynolds, handing over the envelope to his superior.

Ravenscroft tore open the envelope and read its contents. 'This is just as I thought, Tom. *Regret to inform you that we have no one in our company by the name of Anstruther. You must be mistaken. Irving.* So, Anstruther was lying to us yet again. We had better have him in. Bring him to the interview-room, Reynolds.'

'Right, sir,' replied the constable, closing his ledger and leaving the room.

'This would more than seem to confirm his guilt. First he says he is a major in the Guards, then an actor in Sir Henry Irving's company. The man has told us a tissue of lies from beginning to end, and I mean to get to the bottom of all this once and for all,' said an angry Ravenscroft.

'You better come quickly, sir,' said a breathless Reynolds, rushing into the room. 'Something has happened to the prisoner!'

The three men quickly made their way down the long damp corridor, Ravenscroft leading the way into the open cell.

'Good grief!' exclaimed Crabb, as Ravenscroft knelt down by the figure that lay on the floor.

'Is he—?' began Reynolds, hovering near the doorway.

'Dead, I'm afraid. When was the last time you checked on the prisoner, Reynolds?' asked Ravenscroft studying the dead man.

'When I brought in his food, just after twelve,' replied the constable, looking anxious.

'I would say then that he has been dead for at least two hours. He looks as though he died in some agony by the look of him; see how he has clasped his chest as he fell onto the floor.'

'Must have had a seizure of some kind,' offered Crabb.

'I would have thought he was far too young and healthy for that. Is this the dinner you brought in?' asked Ravenscroft, turning to the half-empty plate of food.

'Yes, sir.'

'He must have been eating it when he fell ill. Although the plate is still on the table, the utensils appear to have been dropped on to the floor.'

'You think he could have been poisoned?' asked Crabb.

'That must remain a strong possibility,' said Ravenscroft, smelling the remaining food on the plate.

'Mutton pie, and two vegetables, I believe, sir. Nearly took a mouthful of it myself, only Mrs Reynolds usually makes up some sandwiches for my lunch. Very good at making sandwiches is Mrs Reynolds. Cheese and pickle is her speciality, and very good it is as well.'

'Yes, thank you, Reynolds,' said Ravenscroft annoyed, 'Go and fetch the doctor right away and lock the station door behind you; we don't want anyone wandering in here.'

'Yes, sir.'

'And, Reynolds, where did this food come from?'

'From the Hop Pole, sir. The boy bought it over here.'

'Right. You can go now, Reynolds, and hurry back.'

'Yes, sir.'

'Well, Tom, what do you make of this?' asked Ravenscroft.

'Could have been poisoned I suppose.'

'It looks that way, but why was he poisoned? If Anstruther was responsible for the deaths of Hollinger and the man in the abbey, why was he killed? It appears to be beyond any understanding,' said a bewildered Ravenscroft.

'Perhaps he was innocent after all,' suggested Crabb.

'You may be right, in which case all that he told us about his desire to leave the Hop Pole that night must have been true, although he certainly lied about his profession. But if that was the case, why was he killed?'

'He could have had an accomplice.'

'You mean Ross, or someone else, who decided to kill him to prevent him discovering the resting place of the golden goblet. The killer wanted the treasure for himself, but if that was the case, then why not go and just recover the treasure for yourself rather than bother with killing Anstruther? It just does not make any sense — unless of course, Anstruther was killed to prevent him telling us what he knew. If he did have an accomplice that would explain why he was silenced before he could speak out and implicate him.'

'He could have killed himself, took poison like.'

'Anstruther did not strike me as the kind of person who would have taken his own life. If we assume that Anstruther was entirely innocent, then perhaps he had come across something that the murderer did not want us to know, and that was why he was killed.'

'I'm afraid you have lost me,' said Crabb, scratching his head.

'No matter. We may be getting ahead of ourselves. Anstruther might not have been poisoned at all. He could have died of natural causes, although I doubt it. One thing we can do, after Reynolds has returned with the doctor, is trace the route of that food back to the Hop Pole.'

* * *

A few minutes later, Ravenscroft and Crabb found themselves standing in the busy kitchens of the Hop Pole.

'I can assure you that there is nothing wrong with our mutton pie,' said the landlord. 'I've served three portions of it today to customers, and no one has complained of feeling ill.'

'That's as maybe, but I need to have a word with the boy who delivered the food,' demanded Ravenscroft, placing the half eaten plate of food on one of the tables behind him.

'Stebbins!' shouted the landlord.

'Stebbins? Did you say Stebbins? I know that name,' said Ravenscroft.

A young lad of around twelve years of age quickly entered the kitchens. 'Why, bless my soul, if it ain't Mr Ravenscroft again.'

'How do you do, Stebbins? It must be a year or more since I saw you last at the Tudor in Malvern.'

'And a right time we had of it as well, sir,' grinned the young man.

'I did not know that you had a position here. I've not seen you around the Hop Pole,' enquired Ravenscroft.

'Been away for the past week, sir, visiting me aunt in Bromyard, she be all cubbed up.'

'Cubbed up?' asked Ravenscroft.

'Bent badly, sir, to say nothing of her tissick.'

'Tissick?'

'Bad cough.'

'So when did you return here?' asked Ravenscroft becoming irritated.

'Came back early this morning. Heard you was on the case, Mr Ravenscroft. Knew it would not be long before we became reacquainted like.'

'And how long have you been employed here, Stebbins?'

'Since Christmas, sir. Got a bit tired of all them old folks coming to Malvern to take the water cure. Fussy old lot. Always complaining about the food and the hills. Moan all day long they did. No matter what you did for them, they was never satisfied. Tight as well, the majority of 'em. Tips was no good. Not enough to feed a church mouse. More interesting clientele 'ere, sir.'

'Tell me, Stebbins, what happened this morning when you took the food to the prisoner?' asked Ravenscroft.

'Something afoot then?'

'Just answer the question, Stebbins.'

'Well, your constable comes across about ten and says he wants some food for his gent in the cells, and I was to bring it across at twelve.'

'And?'

'Well, that's what I did. I took the food across to the station just after twelve.'

'You collected the food from in here?'

'Yes, sir. Cook served it up on a plate. I put it on a tray, covered it over with a cloth, and I took it across, sharp like.'

'Now, Stebbins, this is most important. When you took the food across, did you stop anywhere, speak to anyone, or put the tray down?' asked Ravenscroft, a serious expression on his face.

'No, Mr Ravenscroft. I went straight there and delivered the food to Constable Reynolds.'

'Are you sure on that point, my lad?' asked Crabb, looking puzzled.

'Cross me heart, and tell you no lies, gents,' replied a straight-faced Stebbins, crossing himself.

'What about the jug of ale?' asked Ravenscroft, after a moment's deliberation.

'Didn't take him no ale.'

'What ale, sir?' enquired Crabb.

'There was a jug on the table in the cell. Thank you, Stebbins, that will be all for now.'

'Right you are, sir. If you wants to know anything else, you just lets us know. Stebbins is your man.'

'I will remember that,' smiled Ravenscroft.

'I'll keep a look out and let you know if I hears anything,' said the grinning youth as he left the room, followed by the landlord.

'You do that, Stebbins. I will be obliged,' shouted Ravenscroft.

'Well, sir. Looks as though it wasn't the mutton pie that killed him then,' said Crabb.

'I sincerely hope not, or we will be in serious trouble. Whilst we have been busily engaged in talking to Stebbins, that cat over there has just finished off the remains of that pie!'

* * *

'Now then, Reynolds, tell me about the ale,' asked Ravenscroft, after he and Crabb had hastily returned to the station.

'What ale, sir?'

'The ale that was delivered to the prisoner, man. I clearly saw a jug on the table in the cell. Did it arrive with the food?'

'No, sir. The lad brought in the food, and left it on the counter.'

'And then?'

'Well, I took it down to the cells and gave it to the prisoner.'

'And the jug of ale?'

'That was on the counter when I come back.'

'Let's get this right, Reynolds. You took the food down to the prisoner and when you returned you found the jug of ale on the counter.'

'That's correct. I just assumed that the lad had forgotten it, and had returned with it during my absence,' replied a perplexed Reynolds, becoming increasingly redder in the face.

'And what did you do next?' asked Crabb.

'I took it down to the prisoner.'

'How long were you away giving the prisoner his food?' asked Ravenscroft.

'About ten minutes, sir. Prisoner wanted to know what was going on, and where you were, so I told him.'

'Where is this jug and its remains now?'

'I washed them up, sir. There was only a bit left in the bottom. Gone off, I'd say, so I threw it away.'

'Thank you, Reynolds,' sighed Ravenscroft.

'Must have been the ale then, sir,' said Crabb.

'It appears that way. Whoever killed Anstruther must have known that you would have taken the food down to the prisoner, Reynolds, and all he had to do was wait until the room was empty and place the jug on the counter. You are sure you saw no one entering or leaving the building at around that time?'

'No, sir. I'm sorry,' replied the crestfallen policeman.

'What now, sir?' asked Crabb.

'Let us go and break the news to the rest of the party.'

* * *

'Good heavens!' exclaimed Ganniford.

Ravenscroft and Crabb had just revealed the news of Anstruther's demise to Miss Eames, Ganniford and Jenkins in the snug of the Hop Pole.

'So you see why I cannot permit any of you to leave until this matter has been cleared up,' said Ravenscroft, standing with his back to the fire.

'What a terrible thing to happen,' said Miss Eames, bringing a handkerchief to her eyes.

'But why, Inspector? Why would anyone want to harm the major?' asked Jenkins, sitting back in his armchair, and peering at Ravenscroft through his spectacles with a look of incredulity.

'That is what I am trying to find out,' replied Ravenscroft.

'It must have been that fellow Ross. He must be behind all this. Killed poor Hollinger and now Anstruther,' said Ganniford, standing behind Miss Eames and placing a comforting hand on her shoulder.

'Oh, why do you say that?' asked Ravenscroft.

'It stands to sense. If we are all direct descendants of this Roger de la Pole fellow, then if we find the treasure there will be less of us to take a share in the proceeds.'

'Do you have to put it so crudely, my dear Ganniford?' reprimanded Jenkins.

'Well, I certainly didn't kill the two gentlemen, and I know that you are above such things, Jenkins, and Miss Eames is a lady beyond reproach. So that only leaves Ross. It's as plain as a pikestaff that he must be your killer, Ravenscroft — and the sooner you make a greater effort to find the criminal, the sooner we can all depart from this wretched town,' continued Ganniford.

'I think you are being too harsh with the inspector,' interjected Jenkins.

'I can assure you that I have the police forces in three counties on the look-out for the man. It can only be a matter of time before he is sighted and an arrest is made.'

'I wish I had your confidence,' grumbled Ganniford, returning to his seat.

'I have to tell you that Anstruther was not a member of Her Majesty's Army, as he claimed. In fact, he declared himself to be an actor by profession, no less than a member of Henry Irving's famous Lyceum Theatre Company in

London, but I'm afraid that even this turned out to be a lie. Did Anstruther ever say anything to any of you to suggest that he was not whom he seemed?' asked Ravenscroft.

'Told you so, Jenkins!' exclaimed Ganniford. 'I told you there was something decidedly fishy about that man.'

'Anything in particular, sir?'

Ganniford merely shrugged his shoulders and turned away.

'Mr Jenkins, if I may turn to you. Something you said has been of a concern to me,' said Ravenscroft addressing the learned scholar.

'Please ask, Inspector. Anything I can do to help,' replied Jenkins forcing a brief smile.

'Why did you go to Trent's house that night?'

'To ensure that the building would be open at twelve that evening.'

'But why did you take it upon yourself to do so? Surely the man Crosbie would have made that arrangement?'

'When Crosbie wrote to me, giving details of the place and time of our meeting, he gave instructions for me to secure the opening of the abbey for our visit at twelve that evening. I was merely following his request,' replied Jenkins, in his calm, methodical manner.

'Do you have the letter on you now, sir?' asked Crabb.

'Of course not. I either destroyed it, or I may have it amongst my papers at home.'

'And yet Trent did not follow your request,' continued Ravenscroft.

'He obviously thought better of it.'

'Strange then that the abbey was open when you all arrived.'

'I was not responsible for that.'

'Can I ask what each of you was doing between the hours of eleven-thirty and twelve-thirty this morning?' asked Ravenscroft, changing the subject of his questioning.

'Mr Ganniford and I were talking together in the lounge,' offered Miss Eames replacing her handkerchief in her sleeve.

'And you, Mr Jenkins?'

'I was visiting the abbey studying the various artefacts there and trying yet again to work out what the strange lettering on the side of the tomb meant.'

'And were you successful?'

'I'm afraid not.'

'How long were you there?'

'Just over an hour. I returned here for lunch just before one.'

'Did anyone see you there inside the abbey?'

'Look here, Ravenscroft, what are you suggesting?' interrupted Ganniford.

'I am not suggesting anything, Mr Ganniford. We know that someone delivered a jug of poisoned ale to the police station just after twelve this morning. I was merely trying to establish where you all were at that time.'

'To answer your question, Inspector, I believe I was quite alone in the abbey. I remember thinking how peaceful and calm everything was there.'

'Thank you, Mr Jenkins.'

'Look, Ravenscroft, surely you will allow us all to leave now. You can see we have nothing to do with these awful murders,' protested Ganniford.

'I think it would be better if we remained, Ganniford,' said Jenkins. 'After all, we have not yet recovered the golden goblet.'

'Little chance of that, unless you can find out what those letters mean on the side of the tomb,' grumbled Ganniford.

'Nathaniel, I think we should try and do all we can to assist the inspector,' said Miss Eames, trying to placate her companion.

'If you will excuse us, gentlemen, Miss Eames, my constable and myself have business to attend to,' said Ravenscroft walking briskly out of the room.

* * *

'You think one of them committed these murders?' asked Crabb, as he and Ravenscroft stood outside the Hop Pole.

'Jenkins certainly had the opportunity to deliver the poisoned ale. I don't particularly like the man. He is one of those people who always thinks that he is superior in intelligence to you, and is not reticent in disguising it.'

'What about Ganniford and Miss Eames? They seem quite close.'

'They say they were talking together when the ale was delivered to the station, so neither one, nor the other, had the opportunity to act independently. Of course, they could be in it together.'

'Bit unlikely, sir.'

'Nothing is impossible, Crabb. Six people all told that they are heirs of the Crusader knight, Sir Roger de la Pole, visiting the town in the expectation of recovering the golden goblet — and now two of them and the man who led them here are all dead, and another member of their group has gone missing. I believe it highly possible that Hollinger had worked out the lettering on the side of the tomb, and that he and Anstruther made plans to seek out the treasure together, but that their conversation in the snug of the Hop Pole that night was overheard by a third person, who then decided to kill them so that he could obtain the treasure for himself.'

'What do we do next?'

'I will go and tell Constable Reynolds to keep a keen eye on our three friends. We don't want any of them taking it into their heads to make a sudden departure from the town. You bring round the trap.'

'Oh, where are we going, sir?'

'To the small Gloucestershire village of Meysey Hampton. That is where the letters and numbers on the side of the tomb are directing us to. That is where the golden goblet is hidden — and that is where I believe our killer might well be making for.'

* * *

Their journey was along country lanes, then around the town of Cheltenham, before a steep climb bought them to the top of a large hill which commanded picturesque views over the Gloucestershire countryside. From here the trap made its way through a number of sleepy villages until an old fingerpost indicated that the town of Cirencester was shortly within reach. Presently the tower of the ancient church came into view casting a stately presence over the surrounding countryside.

'I believe that if we take the road to the left that should bring us to the village of Meysey Hampton,' said Ravenscroft, consulting the map on his knees.

The winding lane progressed through the villages with strange sounding names such as Ampney Crucis, Ampney St. Peter and Poulton. Here the stone-built cottages with their neat gardens stood quiet and dignified, in a landscape that seemed, to Ravenscroft, to have stood still through the centuries. Occasionally a lone woman or old man would caste a glance at the passing trap, before resuming their occupations in the fields and hedgerows.

'This must the village,' said Ravenscroft. 'Pull up there and I'll ask that fellow where we might find the church.'

The old man surveyed the two men for a few seconds before indicating with his hand that they were to proceed further down the lane.

Passing by a number of old stone cottages which faced one another across the road, then a large manor house and what Ravenscroft supposed to be the village school, Crabb eventually pulled up the horse outside the church.

'What a pleasant, sleepy village,' remarked Ravenscroft, dismounting from the trap. 'And this must be the Templar church of St Mary's, I believe.'

'You think we might find what we are looking for here, sir?'

'We know that the coded letters on the side of Sir Roger's tomb spelt out the words "Meysey Hampton" and that this church was built at the time of the Templars, so we can only hope that Sir Roger was directing us here with some purpose in mind.'

Ravenscroft walked up the path, entered the porch and pushed open the heavy door, which led into the nave of the church.

'What are we looking for exactly?' asked Crabb.

'I wish I knew. All I know is that there must be something here that relates to Sir Roger.'

'Can I be of assistance to you, gentlemen?' asked an elderly figure in clerical attire who emerged from the main body of the church.

'Good morning to you, sir,' said Ravenscroft. 'You must be the incumbent?'

'I am indeed. The Reverend Thomas Anson at your service, gentlemen,' replied the clergyman, coming forward and shaking Ravenscroft's hand. 'I see that your companion is dressed in police attire.'

'Indeed. This is Constable Crabb and I am Inspector Ravenscroft of the Ledbury Constabulary.'

'You are a far way from home, gentlemen. What brings you to our humble church?'

'We understand that your church was built by the Templars?'

'That could be the case, although some believe that the church might have been founded by either the de Meysey family, or the de Clares. Both were prominent local landowners. No one can be absolutely sure. It was such a long time ago, as I am sure you must appreciate.'

'Which are the oldest parts of the church?' asked Ravenscroft.

'The nave, south transept and, of course, the chancel, are all that remain of the original building. The north transept was completely rebuilt recently in 1874, just before I came here, and the vestry was also added at that date. The most interesting part of the church is the chancel.'

'May we take a look, Vicar?'

'Of course. If you would care to follow me.'

Ravenscroft and Crabb followed the clergyman into the chancel.

'We have some remarkable early glass remaining in the windows here,' said Anson pointing up at the glass picture in the quatrefoil. 'Saint Michael weighing souls.'

'It is very fine and colourful, Vicar. You are fortunate indeed to have such a work still in your church. And how old is the glass?' asked Ravenscroft.

'Fourteenth century. It is quite rare to find glass as early as that these days. Unfortunately the Puritans destroyed quite a lot of early glass in many churches in the seventeenth century, so we are quite fortunate, as you say, that it remained untouched during the troubles.'

'Do you have anything earlier than that in the church? We are looking for anything that might have some association with Sir Roger de la Pole. He was one of the Templar crusader knights,' explained Ravenscroft.

'Sir Roger de la Pole? I cannot recall the name,' replied the clergyman looking deep in thought.

'He is buried in Tewkesbury Abbey,' added Crabb.

'Ah yes, I think I do recall seeing his tomb on my last visit there. It has some rather unusual lettering on its side.'

'That is so, Reverend. We believe that when Sir Roger returned from the Holy Land he bought a golden goblet with him which he took great pains to hide before his death,' said Ravenscroft.

'I see — but I don't understand why you have come here?'

'Professor Salt of Oxford University was able to translate the coded letters on the side of Sir Roger's tomb. They spelt out the name "Meysey Hampton".'

'And you think that because this is probably a Templar church, he could have hidden this goblet here?'

'That is correct.'

'Well, I do not think I can help you. I have never come across anything relating to Sir Roger, and when the old side chapel was demolished, and the north transept rebuilt a few years ago, we found nothing of interest. There was certainly no treasure of any kind.'

'I see,' said Ravenscroft, looking around him at various parts of the building. 'And you have nothing earlier than the windows?'

'Not really, unless you consider the old tomb over there,' replied the clergyman pointing to a raised structure in one corner of the chancel. 'As you can see it is quite plain, no decoration, no lettering, or anything to tell us who might be buried inside.'

'And you have no idea whether it is thirteenth century or not?' asked Ravenscroft walking over to the tomb.

'We have no way of telling its age, but we believe it is very early. Its plainness and lack of ornamentation is in complete contrast to the fine decorated stonework of the rest of the chancel.'

'It must be very unusual for it to be so plain, and giving no indication as to who is laid to rest here,' said Ravenscroft, examining the tomb.

'Early stone tombs can often be plain and simple, almost as though the person buried there had given precise instructions that his final resting place should emphasize the austerity and chastity of his life on earth.'

'Has the tomb ever been opened?' asked Crabb.

'Good Lord! Not to my knowledge. Why would anyone want to do such a thing?' exclaimed Anson.

'Can you tell me whether you have had any recent visitors to the church? Perhaps someone making similar enquiries and taking a particular interest in this tomb?' suggested Ravenscroft.

'No. I don't think I recall anyone at all visiting the church in the past few weeks. We lead a very quiet life here. I believe our last visitors were here at Christmas.'

'That is very interesting, Vicar. Has there been anyone visiting the village recently?'

'No one, Inspector.'

'Thank you. Well this is all very puzzling, Crabb. Can I ask what those scratch marks are on the wall above the tomb?' asked Ravenscroft.

'They were probably made by one of the masons who constructed the chancel. Medieval workmen often liked to leave some sign of their handiwork, so that future generations would know of their creation.'

'See here, Crabb. Run your hand over the indentations and tell me what you can make out?' instructed an excited Ravenscroft, after a few seconds.

'This feels like an "R",' said Crabb.

'And the other?'

'A "P".'

'Exactly! The "R" could stand for "Roger" and the "P" for "Pole". Roger de la Pole.'

'Fascinating,' said the vicar. 'I have always wondered what the letters were and what they meant.'

'I think that Sir Roger, by making sure that the letters R and P were inscribed on the wall directly above the tomb, was indicating that this may be the final resting place of the goblet. Reverend, do you think it would be possible for us to open the tomb?'

'Good Heavens — if you will excuse the expression. I cannot under any circumstances permit that violation,' protested Anson, throwing up his arms in horror.

'I am sorry to cause offence. Nevertheless, I believe that it is imperative that we recover whatever is inside the tomb. If the golden goblet is found inside there, then we can ensure that it is displayed in a museum, where it would not only be secure but where its full glory could be enjoyed by everyone. If it is left inside, there is always the danger that someone, entirely lacking in scruples, may uncover the secret of the letters, and will violate the shrine,' said Ravenscroft, trying to sound as persuasive as he could.

'I appreciate what you are saying. Inspector. It would indeed be a terrible thing if the tomb was to be broken into, but I'm afraid I cannot give you the permission you require. All I can suggest is that if you write and explain your request to the Bishop of Gloucester and the Church Commissioners, they might allow you to proceed. If that permission is granted, then I would offer no objection.'

'Thank you, Reverend. I quite understand your position. We will indeed approach the correct authorities. In the meantime, until we are able to return, we believe it is possible that some mischievous person may attempt to break into the tomb, and accordingly I would suggest that you lock the building at all times, except, of course, when you are conducting church services.'

'Certainly, Inspector, I will be more than pleased to undertake your request.'

'And if you could keep a look-out for any strangers in the vicinity and let us know if there are any,' said Ravenscroft handing the clergyman one of his cards.

'Yes, yes, of course.'

'Thank you, Reverend. I will write to the bishop today. Until we are able to return, I wish you a very good day.'

CHAPTER NINE

LEDBURY

Ravenscroft sealed the envelope, let out a deep sigh and leaned back in his armchair. The light from the candle on his desk fell on his pocket watch and he noted that the time had shortly passed the hour of five in the morning.

He had spent a restless night and, being unable to sleep, had risen reluctantly from his bed and had made his way down the stairs to the main room of the house where he had busied himself in composing a letter to the Bishop of Gloucester setting out the full facts of the case, and putting forward his request to open the unmarked tomb. Now at last that duty had been done and he could turn his mind to other matters.

Ross was dead. There was no doubt about it. Killed in a shooting accident they said ten years ago. Yet he and Crabb had interviewed the Scotsman in his own house, and he had been very much alive. Crabb had joked that it had been the ghost of the dead man who had spoken to them, but he did not believe in such fanciful nonsense. Anyway, Ross had also been seen by others that night at the abbey, albeit only fleetingly, before he had quit the scene. Ross was dead. Ross was alive.

He knew that unless the man was apprehended within the next few hours, he would feel compelled to let the others leave the town, and with their departure might go any hope he had of arriving at the truth of the matter. There still remained the possibility, of course, that Ross was entirely innocent, and that either Jenkins, Ganniford or Miss Eames, either acting alone, or as a group, had committed the crimes in their desire to find the resting place of the goblet for themselves.

Then there was Professor Salt's telegram, which had been waiting for him at the station in Tewkesbury when he and Crabb had returned late that night from their excursion to Meysey Hampton — *Regret to inform you no living descendants of Sir Roger de la Pole. Had one son who died in infancy. Salt.*- it had said, the starkness of its words adding yet further to his gloom. So none of the group would have a claim on the treasure should it ever be found. Either the man Crosbie had created the fake chart to make them each believe that they were the true descendants of the old Templar Knight, or the whole story had been yet one more untruthful layer in a mountain of lies. He would have to confront the three remaining members of the group in the morning in a final attempt to obtain the truth.

As Ravenscroft looked into the flame of the flickering candle, he wondered whether he would ever solve the case. Would he ever be able to obtain justice for Hollinger, Anstruther and the man in the open coffin? Despite his apparent death ten years before, Ross had to be his chief suspect, but the wretched man was still out there somewhere and could not be found.

In little over an hour dawn would break and with the coming of the new day there would be new endeavour and with it new hope.

* * *

'Good morning to you, sir, Mrs Ravenscroft,' said Crab entering the room cheerfully.

'Good morning, Tom. Do draw up a chair and help yourself to some tea and toast,' said Lucy.

'Thank you, ma'am,' replied the constable, seating himself at the table.

'Well, Tom, what news do you bring?' asked Ravenscroft laying down his newspaper.

'Unfortunately nothing, sir. I have just called in at the station, and I'm afraid that there is nothing at all to report. The men have made extensive enquiries in the three counties but there have been no reported sightings of Ross,' said Crabb, reaching for the toast rack.

'Damn the man! Where the devil has he got to?' said an impatient Ravenscroft. 'Why has no one reported seeing him?'

'He could be out on Bredon Hill somewhere, or in one of the nearby villages. I could send out some men to scour the hills,' suggested Crabb, before taking a mouthful of toast and marmalade.

'Do as you wish,' sighed Ravenscroft. 'It can do no harm.'

'Perhaps the men may soon discover the whereabouts of your mysterious Mr Ross,' said Lucy trying to sound optimistic.

'We shall have to let Ganniford, Jenkins and Miss Eames go this morning unless there are more lies to unravel,' said Ravenscroft gloomily.

'Things are sometimes never what they seem,' remarked Lucy pouring out some more tea.

'All this is confoundedly annoying — what was that you just said?' said Ravenscroft, turning quickly towards his wife.

'Things are sometimes never what they seem,' repeated Lucy.

'That is it!' exclaimed Ravenscroft. 'We have been assuming all along that Crosbie, Anstruther and Hollinger were murdered so that their killer could acquire the treasure for himself. We know that Crosbie had met each of our six members in turn, showing them some made-up chart which purported to show that they were all descended from Sir Roger de la Pole, and had enticed them to meet him in Tewkesbury in order to find the missing goblet — but why do that? Why not seek out the treasure for yourself? Why involve six complete strangers in your search?'

'Perhaps he thought they might be able to translate the lettering on the side of the coffin, where he had failed,' suggested Lucy, leaning forward.

'But there would have been no guarantee of that. After all, many people have read the inscription down through the centuries and yet not one of them, we presume, has ever succeeded.'

'Your Professor Salt was able to arrive at the solution,' added Crabb.

'Yes, but Salt is a medieval scholar, schooled in such learning; a brilliant mind who saw in a flash of inspiration how the code might be solved. Up until now we had assumed that the man Crosbie had been killed by his accomplice after he had found something inside the tomb, and at first we had thought that the tomb had contained the golden goblet. We know now, however, that was not so, otherwise the killer would have fled the scene taking the treasure with him. Secondly, we assumed that Hollinger had worked out what the letters stood for, and had imparted that knowledge to Anstruther in the snug of the Hop Pole that night, and that our killer had overheard them, and decided to kill them to acquire and keep that knowledge for himself. At first we thought that Anstruther killed Hollinger and that he had then made a hasty departure before the body was discovered — but then if he was the killer why would he have gone in the opposite direction to where the treasure was hidden? It doesn't make sense. Then we assumed that Anstruther was poisoned because he, too, knew where the treasure was, and our killer had to ensure that he was put out of the way before he revealed all. But if Anstruther had not been party to the secret, why was he poisoned? The more one continues to look at all this, the more we keep going round in circles, and the answers keep evading us. Things are not as they seem, that is what you said, my dear. What if Crosbie, Hollinger and Anstruther were killed for an entirely different reason, one which is not yet apparent — and what if the whole story about the Templar and his missing treasure has been a complete diversion?' said Ravenscroft, warming to his subject.

'But we found the marks above the tomb at Meysey Hampton,' interrupted Crabb, a puzzled expression on his face.

'Indeed, that much is confirmed. Perhaps there is a treasure, but what if the summoning of our six people to Tewkesbury had nothing to do with the finding of that prize? What if they were enticed here for an entirely different reason?'

'I don't see what you are getting at, sir,' said Crabb, buttering yet another slice of toast.

'Go on,' said Lucy, encouraging her husband.

'Six strangers each believing that they had journeyed to Tewkesbury to inherit that which they thought was rightfully theirs to claim. No, the answer to this mystery lies elsewhere. I am sure the solution has something to do with the man Ross. What if Ross is behind all this? What if he and Crosbie stumbled across the old story about the Templar Knight and saw a way in which they could use it to bring the others to the town?'

'But why?' asked Crabb.

'That is what we have to find out.'

'Begging your pardon, sir, but we don't even know if Ross is dead or alive.'

'Precisely — and that is why we need to find out whether Ross was really killed in that shooting accident all those years ago.'

'And how will you do that?' asked Lucy.

'Eat up your breakfast, Tom, then you and I will seek out the newspaper archives at the local library. Almost certainly the newspapers of the day would have reported the case and the inquest. That is where the answer to all this may be found.'

* * *

'Good morning to you, sir, I believe your library may contain back copies of the local newspaper,' said Ravenscroft, addressing the grey-haired librarian who was seated behind a large desk scattered with piles of books.

'Oh, I would not know whether that is the case, or no,' replied the man, turning over a page of one of the open volumes.

'We were given to understand that we might find back issues of *The Evesham Journal* here.'

'I would not be sure on that rash assumption, my dear sir. No, not at all. Dear me, no. May I be so bold as to enquire who is requesting such material?' asked the librarian looking up from his studies and peering over his spectacles at the two men.

'Inspector Ravenscroft — and this is Constable Crabb.'

'I see. Can't help you I'm afraid. No, cannot be of any assistance whatsoever,' replied the man, resuming his reading.

'Do you, or do you not, have back copies of *The Evesham Journal* within the confines of this library?' asked Ravenscroft irritably.

'*Confines* you say? What an unusual expression to use on such a day. Very neat indeed. You could have used interior, or even inside, or some other expression of equal meaning, but, no, you chose confines. Such an unusual word. *Confines.* Yes indeed.'

'Look here, do you have the back issues of *The Evesham Journal* in this library, or not? I would be obliged for a straight answer,' said Ravenscroft, more and more annoyed by the librarian's strange manner.

'*Obliged* for an answer, my dear sir? Would that I could give you an answer. Dear me, no. I can give you one answer, but then that may not be the correct one. Then I could give you another answer, and that may well prove to be the one you are looking for. But then indeed it may not. You see my predicament.'

'Will you answer my question?' said Ravenscroft raising his voice.

'There is no need for annoyance. Annoyance will get you nowhere. Dear me, no. Annoyance will not do at all. No, it will not.'

'The man speaks in riddles, sir,' muttered Crabb.

'If you do not answer my question, then I will search every inch of this library until I find what I am looking for,' said Ravenscroft, leaning forward until he towered over the little man.

'That would be extremely unwise, my dear sir. Extremely unwise indeed. Dear me no, that just won't do at all. Not at all. That is not to be borne. Indeed not.'

'Then you leave me no choice. Lead on, Crabb. We will turn this library upside down until we find what we are looking for,' said Ravenscroft angrily brushing aside the other's comments.

'Right you are, sir,' said Crabb, adopting a business-like tone.

'*Evesham Journal* you say? If you would care to accompany me, gentlemen, you will soon be aware of my predicament,' said the librarian, rising hastily from his chair and crossing over towards a large oak door at the other side of the room. '*Evesham Journal*. Well I never. No one ever asks to see that. No one at all.'

'Well *I* am asking. It is a matter of the gravest importance,' said Ravenscroft sternly.

'Gravest importance you say. Then I suppose it may be to some people. To others it is apparently not, for had it been so, we would have had a far greater number of enquiries for such material over the years. Indeed we would,' said the man unlocking the door with a large, rusty, iron key.

Ravenscroft sighed and gave Crabb a look of frustration.

'There, my dear sir!' exclaimed the librarian pulling open the door of the room.

'Good heavens!' exclaimed Crabb, staring at the piles of books and papers that seemed to occupy each inch of the darkened room.

'Now you see my predicament,' said the librarian, nodding his head from side to side.

'I do indeed,' sympathized Ravenscroft.

'I believe you might well find what you are looking for here — but then again you might not.'

'Can you bring us a candle?' asked Ravenscroft. 'It is very dark in here.'

'A candle? And where might I obtain such an item, I should like to know? Then indeed if I were to acquire the said requested item, it could prove of a dangerous nature with so much combustible material at our disposal. No, sir, a candle is not to be advised at all, even if one could be located. No, not at all. Dear me, no.'

'No matter, sir,' said Crabb, edging himself between several piles of books and opening a small window on the other side of the room.

'How extraordinary!' exclaimed the librarian. 'No one has ever opened that window for as long as I can remember. No, they have not.'

'Well done, Crabb. Might I suggest that you leave my constable and I free to find what we are looking for?' suggested Ravenscroft. 'I am sure you must be greatly occupied with your books, and we would not wish to take up any more of your time than is absolutely necessary.'

'Indeed I am, sir. Busy indeed. I wish you well in your endeavours,' said the man forcing a brief smile before he left the room.

'Close the door, Tom. I think we might do a lot better on our own, and without interruption.'

'Right, sir,' said Crabb closing the door.

'What an irritating little man.'

'Where do we begin?'

'I would think that the past copies of *The Evesham Journal*, would have been bound. I know it is the custom for such newspaper companies and librarian to bind their past issues into six-monthly periods.'

'Right, sir,' replied Crabb making his way between the stacks of books.

'I'll take this side of the room.'

The two men worked their way through the piles of books, until Crabb let out a sudden cry, '*Evesham Journal,* sir!'

'Well done, Tom.'

'What year are we looking for?'

'If the shooting accident happened approximately ten years ago, then we need to look for the year 1879.'

Crabb attacked the large pile of books, displacing many of the heavy volumes on the floor beside him. 'Here we are. 1879. Runs to two volumes.'

'Each volume must cover six months of the year. You take that one, and I will take this one.'

The two men carried the two volumes into the main room of the library.

'Ah, I see, gentlemen, that you must have found what you were seeking,' said the librarian looking up from his desk.

'Indeed so,' said Ravenscroft, placing his volume down on one of the tables. 'You take the other volume, Crabb, and see if you can find any reports of shooting accidents.'

The two men worked in silence for some minutes, before Ravenscroft suddenly called out, 'Over here, Tom!'

Crabb looked over his superior's shoulder, as Ravenscroft read aloud from the newspaper:

> *INQUEST HELD REGARDING DEATH OF LOCAL LANDOWNER.*
>
> *The inquest was held yesterday at the Star and Garter Inn regarding the death of local landowner, Mr Charles Ross, who met with a fatal shooting accident last Saturday morning, whilst staying at the residence of Lord Ernest Treaves of Elmley Castle.*
>
> *Lord Treaves stated that the deceased had been one of a number of guests who had been staying at his house for the weekend. Although his lordship did not accompany his guests on the shoot, he confirmed that the party had been in excellent spirits and that Mr Ross had displayed no signs of anxiety or depression.*
>
> *Mr Henry Phillips, gamekeeper to Lord Treaves, gave evidence. He stated that he had left the gentlemen members of the hunting party on the edge of the wood, whilst he went*

off to encourage the beaters to commence their work. Whilst undertaking this, he had heard the sound of a gun being discharged followed by loud shouting. Upon rushing out of the wood, he had found the deceased lying on the ground, by one of the stiles, blood pouring from the side of his head. Shortly afterwards he was joined by the other members of the shooting party. An examination of the body quickly confirmed that Mr Ross was dead. When questioned further by the coroner, Mr Phillips confirmed that he had been the first on the scene and that it was clearly apparent that the deceased had been shot through the side of his temple whilst attempting to climb over a stile.

Doctor Rupert Morrison next gave evidence. He was called to the scene shortly after the accident and found the deceased lying in a pool of blood. It was apparent that the gun had accidentally discharged itself whilst the deceased had been attempting to climb a stile, and that he had been killed instantaneously.

Further evidence was given by other members of the shooting party, who all confirmed the account given by the gamekeeper. The coroner returned a verdict of accidental death. We are given to understand that Mr Charles Ross, whose estates are to be found at Bredon's Norton, was not married and leaves no heirs.

'Well, Tom, what do you make of that?' said Ravenscroft looking up from the newspaper.

'It certainly looks as though our Mr Ross is well and truly dead,' replied Crabb.

'So who was that man we interviewed in the house at Bredon's Norton? If Ross was dead, killed at that hunting party, who was the man we were talking to? I think we need to go and make a call on this Lord Treaves and see what else we can discover about that hunting party,' said Ravenscroft, closing the volume and standing up from the table.

'I see that you have found what you were looking for, gentlemen,' interjected the librarian.

'Yes, indeed. Thank you,' said Ravenscroft, anxious to make his departure.

'I wonder if you would care to return the volumes to the place where you found them, my dear sir,' coughed the librarian. 'I find that the carrying of such heavy tomes is not entirely conducive to my present condition. Indeed it does not. No, not at all.'

'Oh, I'm afraid that will not be possible,' replied Ravenscroft, reaching the door. 'It is a matter of life and death that we leave as quickly as possible.'

'But, sir, if the volumes are not returned to their proper place, no one will ever be able to locate them ever again. That won't do at all. No it will not.'

'As no one has ever requested such material in the past, I very much doubt, my dear sir, that you will be faced with such a difficulty in the future. Good day to you,' shouted Ravenscroft, as he and Crabb stepped out quickly through the door and into the street.

'But, my dear sir, this won't do at all—'

* * *

Thirty minutes later, as Crabb drove the trap up the long driveway, with its neatly cut lawns and flowering shrubs on either side, that gradually wound its up to the front entrance of the imposing Georgian house, Ravenscroft wondered whether he was about to enter yet another darkened alleyway where the truth would seek to elude him once again. The newspaper report had confirmed that Charles Ross had died as the result of a shooting accident, yet it was clear that the man was very much alive, or at the least someone who was pretending to be the deceased man. But if that was the case, why would someone seek to impersonate a corpse? Now that it had been proved that the Templar Knight had left no descendants, there would be little point in anyone trying to convince people that he was Ross, and that de la Pole was his ancestor. Ross's house and lands were also not clearly worth the effort of anyone laying claim to them. They appeared to have stood empty and neglected for the past ten years. There remained the possibility, of course, that someone else after all had been killed in Ross's place — but if that was the case, where had Ross been for the past ten years, and why had he decided to return now? Either way, Ravenscroft knew that he needed to find out more about that hunting party, and the death of one of its number.

'Tidy pile this,' remarked Crabb, pulling up the horse at the front entrance of the building.

'This is how the other half live, Tom.'

'Something like this could be all yours one day, sir, with a bit of luck.'

'I doubt that, Tom, and certainly not on a policeman's humble wage.'

'There's always the horses, sir.'

'I don't think so. A fool and his money are soon parted, as they say. Anyway, I am sure that Mrs Ravenscroft would not approve of such rashness.'

As Ravenscroft alighted from the trap, the door to the house was flung open and a manservant made his way quickly down the steps.

'Good morning, gentlemen.'

'Good morning. We would like to speak to your master,' said Ravenscroft.

'Do you have an appointment, sir?' enquired the servant, casting a cautious eye over the new arrivals.

'No, but I am sure he will see us. We are here on police business. My name is Detective Inspector Ravenscroft and my companion is Constable Crabb.'

'If you would care to follow me, gentlemen, I will see if his lordship is free to see you,' replied the manservant, indicating that the two policemen were to follow him up the steps.

'If you would wait here, gentlemen,' said the manservant, after Ravenscroft and Crabb had entered into the hallway.

'What is it, Spurgeon?' bellowed out a voice from somewhere above them.

'It is the police, your lordship,' said the manservant, as a tall, grey-haired, elderly gentleman wearing a well-worn tweed suit strode down the majestic staircase.

'Lord Treaves?' enquired Ravenscroft.

'Police, you say? I suppose it's those damned poachers again. Told me gamekeeper to deal with them. If you don't keep a firm hand on them, things soon get out of hand. I'm sure my butler can answer any questions you may have,' said the gentleman, turning away briskly and intent on entering one of the adjoining rooms.

'It is not about the poachers, your lordship,' called out Ravenscroft. 'We are here making enquiries about the death of one of your guests.'

'One of my guests? Dead, you say? Can't remember anyone dying recently. Must have the wrong house,' replied Treaves, scratching his head before turning away.

'Mr Charles Ross to be exact,' said Ravenscroft.

'Ross?'

'Charles Ross from Bredon's Norton.'

'Ross. Charles Ross? Been dead for years,' said Treaves, walking into his study.

'That's what we would like to ask you about, if you would be so kind to give my constable and myself a few minutes of your time,' persisted Ravenscroft, following their host into his inner sanctum, where the smell of damp tweed and stale tobacco smoke hung heavily in the air, and where the walls were hung with numerous hunting trophies and faded photographs.

'Why would you want to ask me about Ross? Gave evidence to the coroner all those years ago. All finished with. Nothing else to add,' said Treaves abruptly, pouring himself a drink from one of the decanters on a sideboard.

'Then you can confirm that it was Mr Ross who was killed?'

'Of course I can. I know when I see a dead man, especially when he was one of my guests.'

'I believe he died as the result of a shooting accident.'

'If you know that, why do you need to ask me about it? The man's been dead for best part of ten years. Can't think what you want to know after all this time,' said Treaves draining his glass.

'If you could just tell us what happened in your own words, sir, I would be obliged.'

'Fellow went out hunting with my other guests who were staying with me for the weekend. Didn't go with them; back playing me up that day. Shot whilst climbing over a stile, they said. Must have leaned on his gun and it went off. Nasty business. Blew away the side of his face, I believe. Silly blighter should have been more careful. You have to know what you are doing with guns. They can be dangerous things in the wrong hands. Not my responsibility. You shoot, Ravenscroft?'

'No.'

'You should take it up. Good for the constitution, and helps keep down the vermin,' replied Treaves, stroking his moustache and staring vacantly out of the window.

'You saw the body afterwards?'

'What body?'

'Mr Ross.'

'Oh yes. I told you so. Face blown away. Poor blighter.'

'So it was definitely Ross?'

'Told you so, man. It was Ross,' replied Treaves, expressing a degree of irritation as he replenished his glass from the decanter.

'Was Mr Ross a frequent house guest here?' asked Ravenscroft.

'Not really. I knew he had lands somewhere locally, but I had never mixed with the fellow.'

'So why did you invite him?'

'Blessed if I know now. I suppose someone must have suggested his name to me. Of course, if I'd known all about that business in India beforehand, I would never have had anything to do with him.'

'Oh, what business was that, sir?'

'Fighting those Afghan fellows they were.'

'Could you enlighten us further?' asked Ravenscroft, anxious to know more about this new line in his enquiry.

'Apparently, Ross and his men were escorting a party to one of the hill forts near the Afghan frontier when they were set upon by a group of the savages. All of them were wiped out except for Ross, who was more intent on saving his own skin. Left them all there to die, so they said. Bounder! All came out after his death. As I said, if I'd known beforehand he would certainly have not been invited here, I can tell you!' snorted Treaves, growing red in the face.

'I see,' added Ravenscroft.

'Can't abide socializing with cowards who don't do their duty!'

'Indeed not. Thank you, Lord Treaves, you have been most helpful. I notice that you have a large number of photographs on the walls,' said Ravenscroft.

'Like to take a photograph of all my weekend guests. Pleases the wife, you know. She likes to keep a record of who has been here, if you see what I mean. Got to keep the other half happy. What's it to you?'

'I couldn't help noticing that many of the photographs are of hunting parties. You don't happen to have one of Ross and his companions?' asked Ravenscroft, looking at one of the many framed photographs on the wall.

'Keep most of them in the albums over here,' said Treaves, indicating a large number of books which lay on one of the tables.

'I wonder if we might have a look through them, sir?'

'If you think it will do any good,' said Treaves reluctantly. 'My wife usually writes the dates below each photograph.'

'That is very helpful.' Ravenscroft eagerly turned over the pages of an album which bore the date 1879 on the outside. 'Ah here we are, November 1879.'

'That's Ross there,' said Treaves, looking over Ravenscroft's shoulder, and pointing to one of the dozen or so group of people who had been photographed standing on the steps of the house.

'He certainly looks like the man we interviewed,' said Ravenscroft, looking at the photograph intently. 'Good God! Look, Crabb. If I'm not mistaken, that man there standing to the left of Ross, looks remarkably like Anstruther!'

'I do believe you're correct, sir,' nodded Crabb.

'Major Anstruther you say? It might have been Anstruther who recommended Ross to me as a fellow house guest. Can't think why, especially as they were in the same regiment together. That man standing next to me is their commanding officer, Colonel Eames,' said Treaves.

'Eames!' exclaimed Crabb.

'Miss Eames's late father. Lord Treaves, can you tell us who these two men standing in the back row are?' asked Ravenscroft eagerly.

'That's Ganniford. I was a good friend of his father. We went to the same school together. Believe the other fellow is Jenkins, friend of Ganniford. Recall he was a bit of a dry fish, but comes from a good family, I believe.'

'This is quite fascinating. So Ganniford, Jenkins and Miss Eames's late father were all members of the shooting party,' said Ravenscroft, thinking out loud.

'Blessed if I know why you find all this so interesting,' said Treaves, turning away.

'Just a minute, sir, who is that man at the back, just beginning to face away from the camera?' asked Crabb, pointing to the photograph.

'Could be Hollinger,' answered Ravenscroft bringing the photograph to his face and scrutinizing it once more.

'Oh, that's Hollinger all right,' said Treaves, returning. 'Doctor Andreas Hollinger. Good friend of mine. Lost touch with him a few years ago. He went off to Baden-Baden, or somewhere like that, to look after all them invalids. Haven't seen him since.'

'Lord Treaves, you have been most helpful to us in our enquiries. If you will now excuse us, sir, we have urgent business to attend to. I wish you good day.'

'Glad to have been assistance to you. Got to help the authorities these days, if you can. I'd be obliged if you could do something about those damned poachers.'

'I will endeavour to have a word with the local constabulary,' said Ravenscroft smiling, as he and Crabb left the room.

* * *

'Well, Tom, this changes everything,' said Ravenscroft, as the trap made its way down the winding driveway.

'Strange state of affairs. What was all that about Afghanistan?' asked Crabb.

'Well, it certainly appears that Ross lost his life on that shooting party, and that Ganniford, Jenkins, Hollinger, Anstruther and Miss Eames's late father were all members of the group who went out shooting that day.'

'I thought they all said they had never met each other before, except for Ganniford and Jenkins.'

'That is what they would have us believe. They have sought to spread yet another layer of lies in front of us. It appears, however, that Major Anstruther was a member of Her Majesty's forces after all, despite the fact that he does not appear in the recent Army Lists. Perhaps he left the army some years ago. That would account for the discrepancy. Why then did he tell us all that nonsense about being an actor? Did he do that to lay a false trail? Thought that if we dug too deeply we would reveal his army connections after all? Or was it just bravado on his part? And what were they all doing on that shooting party? Of course! Treaves said that Ross had deserted his post, intent on saving his own life when his companions were killed by those Afghans!'

'Go on,' urged Crabb.

'Don't you see, Tom? It was all a question of honour. That is what this has all been about — nothing to do with the old Templar Knight, or golden goblets. We have been following the wrong path all along. A gentleman's honour! Ross was killed by the other members of the shooting party, because he had left those people to die in Afghanistan all those years ago.'

CHAPTER TEN

TEWKESBURY

As Ravenscroft and Crabb alighted from their trap outside The Hop Pole they were met by an anxious Stebbins.

'Gent gone, sir!' announced the young boy, waving his arms in the air.

'Which gent, Stebbins?' asked Ravenscroft.

'The miserable one with the long nose.'

'Jenkins,' said Crabb.

'Confound it! When?' asked an annoyed Ravenscroft.

'Went after breakfast. Not seen again. Others all in a flap, sir.'

'So Mr Ganniford and Miss Eames are still here?'

'Yes.'

'At least that is something. Do you happen to know where Mr Jenkins went to?'

'No, sir.'

'Thank you, Stebbins. If you hear anything about the missing gent be sure to let us know,' said Ravenscroft, entering the inn.

'I'll ask around. Got me scouts here. Have no fear. Him that's lost will be found. Leave it to Stebbins, sir,' smiled the potboy.

'I sincerely hope so, Stebbins. Where are the others?'

'In the snug.'

Ravenscroft and Crabb entered the small room.

'Thank God, Ravenscroft. You've heard about Jenkins?' said Ganniford, rising from his chair, a worried expression on his face.

'Perhaps you had better tell us what has happened,' suggested Ravenscroft, giving a brief acknowledgement in Miss Eames's direction.

'We all had breakfast together, then Jenkins announced he was going to pay another visit to the abbey and that was the last we saw of him.'

'Did the gentleman say what time he would return?' asked Ravenscroft.

'Mr Jenkins said he would rejoin us for coffee at eleven,' said a nervous Miss Eames.

'I see. It is now half past one,' said Ravenscroft, looking at the old grandfather clock in the corner of the room. 'Has anyone visited the abbey to see if Mr Jenkins is still there?'

'After Mr Jenkins failed to join us, we decided to walk over there to see if some misfortune had befallen him,' replied Miss Eames.

'That clergyman fellow, Jesterson, was there. Said he had been there all morning and that he had seen no sign of Jenkins visiting the building. Seems he never arrived there. Look, Ravenscroft, you must start a search for Jenkins. This is most unlike him to go off on his own like this. I fear something bad could have happened to him,' said Ganniford, becoming agitated.

'Has anyone checked his room?' asked Ravenscroft.

'Why . . . er . . . no. Didn't see the point,' muttered Ganniford.

'Crabb, go and see if Mr Jenkins has returned to his room, and if not, see whether his possessions have gone,' instructed Ravenscroft.

'Don't be silly. Jenkins would not have left without us.'

'Nevertheless, that must remain a possibility. We have to follow all lines of enquiry. Did you report this matter to Constable Reynolds?'

'Your man said he could do nothing until you returned. Where the blazes have you been all morning, Ravenscroft?' grumbled Ganniford.

'Did Mr Jenkins say anything to either of you to suggest that he was going away?' asked Ravenscroft, ignoring the last remark.

'No, nothing, Inspector,' said Miss Eames.

'Nothing. Look, all this is wasting time. Don't you think you should be organizing a search party? Poor Jenkins could be lying injured in some ditch or other, crying out for aid as we speak.'

'We know about Ross and the hunting party,' announced Ravenscroft suddenly.

'What? Er . . . I don't understand,' replied a startled Ganniford.

'This morning my constable and I discovered a newspaper account of the death of Mr Charles Ross at a shooting party ten years ago,' said Ravenscroft, intent on studying the others' reactions to his words.

'But Ross is alive. We all saw him at the abbey. I don't know what you are talking about,' protested Ganniford, turning away.

'It may interest you both to know that we have just visited Lord Treaves at his country residence. He remembers that particular weekend when one of his guests was shot whilst out hunting. He also showed me an interesting photograph of his house party taken at the time. Not only were Major Anstruther and Dr Hollinger present that weekend, but also yourself and Mr Jenkins — and your father, Miss Eames.'

'My father?' asked the startled lady.

'We know all about the attack by the Afghans and how Captain Ross deserted his post,' said Ravenscroft firmly, anxious to press home his advantage.

'This is all gibberish. Don't know what you are talking about,' protested Ganniford.

'The photograph does not lie. What were you all doing there the weekend that Ross was killed?'

'Mr Jenkins is not in his room, sir,' said Crabb suddenly entering the room.

'And what of his possessions?'

'Still there. Nothing has been taken.'

'So, Mr Jenkins did not decide to return to London on his own account.'

'When are you going to start the search?' asked Ganniford, becoming more agitated and growing red in the face.

'When you and Miss Eames start telling us the truth,' retorted Ravenscroft.

'Nothing to tell.'

'Oh, but I think there is a lot to tell, Mr Ganniford. From the start of this investigation you and your friends had us believe that you first met up with one another at the abbey here in Tewkesbury, when in fact all of you, with the exception of Miss Eames, had been present at the shooting party at Lord Treaves's home ten years ago. All that nonsense about six strangers meeting for the first time was just pure invention. What exactly did happen all those years ago? How did Ross die? Was it really an accident — or did you all conspire to end the poor man's life — and if so, why?' said Ravenscroft, confronting Ganniford full in the face.

'It was not like that,' muttered Ganniford, turning away.

'Then what was it like, Mr Ganniford? And you, Miss Eames, you must have known that your father was one of the members of the shooting party? Colonel Eames and Major Hollinger belonged to the same regiment as Charles Ross, and Charles Ross had deserted his post leaving his men, women and children to be slaughtered by the Afghans. That is what all this has been about. A point of honour. Ross was shot as a point of honour — killed because he had deserted his post and bought disgrace upon his regiment,' said Ravenscroft, raising his voice.

'We must tell Inspector Ravenscroft the truth, Nathaniel. We cannot hold out any longer,' said Miss Eames imploringly, looking into Ganniford's eyes.

'Well, Mr Ganniford, are you going to tell us the truth? May I remind you that two of your party are already dead, murdered by an unknown hand, and that a further two members are now missing.'

'All right, all right. Yes, yes, we were all there that weekend, but it is not the way you see it,' said Ganniford.

'Please go on,' urged Ravenscroft.

'We all knew what Ross had done — a despicable act — cowardice of the first order. You are correct when you say that Colonel Eames and Major Anstruther belonged to the same regiment as Ross. What you don't know is that both Jenkins and I had younger brothers who had also been members of the regiment. My own brother was not above eighteen years of age. A mere boy, cut down by those barbarous tribesmen. Ross was in charge that day. He could have saved them, but instead he decided to save his own neck and deserted his post,' said Ganniford with bitterness.

'And Dr Hollinger?' asked Ravenscroft.

'His wife and daughter were also there that day. The girl was just three years of age. Three years of age! An innocent child left to die in that God-forsaken land. My God, Ravenscroft, if you had known what those murdering cutthroats did to them, you would not be standing there today so righteously passing judgement on us.'

'I am not passing judgement, Mr Ganniford. I am merely seeking to ascertain the truth. So that is why you all attended Lord Treaves's party that weekend.'

'We knew that Ross would be there. Our first response was to refuse the invitation, to have nothing more to do with the blackguard, but then there was the regiment's honour to consider. We owed it to the souls of all those dead men, women and children to confront the man.'

'So you shot him whilst out hunting, and made it look like an accident.'

'No, it was not like that. We certainly wanted Ross to pay, but not that way. Death would have been the easy way out for him. We wanted to bring ruin and disgrace on him and his family, make him acknowledge his cowardly actions, to atone for what he had done, but then he cheated us all in the end. Managed to shoot himself whilst climbing over the fence before we could confront him. What justice was there in that?'

'We only have your word for it that Ross died as the result of an accident,' said Ravenscroft.

'You have my word as a gentleman. The others will confirm what I have said.'

'You know that is not possible, sir. Major Anstruther and Dr Hollinger are both dead. Colonel Eames has passed away. That only leaves Mr Jenkins, and he has now gone missing.'

'Then you will have to accept what I have told you. Certainly we wanted to avenge the deaths of those men, women and children, and to confront Ross with his cowardly actions, but, as I said, the man cheated us. Couldn't look after his own gun properly,' said Ganniford sarcastically. 'The stupid man managed to shoot himself in the face whilst climbing over that fence. You may think differently, Inspector, but you will have the deuce to prove otherwise.'

'So why did you all decide to meet again after all these years?' asked Ravenscroft, relieved that he had at last secured the truth.

'After Ross's death, there was nothing else we could do. The matter was closed. The regiment's honour had been preserved. We all went our separate ways, except for Jenkins and myself, who had known one another for some years. Then we were all contacted individually by that man Crosbie, who told us we were all descendants of that de la Pole fellow. The rest you know.'

'You must have felt some unease when you discovered on arrival at the abbey that the other members turned out to be Hollinger and Anstruther?'

'Yes. When Jenkins and myself first met you, my dear lady, the name Eames was familiar to us, but we considered that perhaps you were no relation of our Colonel Eames. When we saw that Hollinger and Anstruther were waiting for us outside the abbey, we thought it best to maintain appearances and create the impression that we had not met before.'

'And Ross? That must have been a shock?' asked Ravenscroft.

'At first when the man appeared outside the abbey, he was wearing a large hat which partially obscured his face, and even when he said his name was Ross I thought he must have been someone else with the same name. Then he was gone, disappeared into the darkness of the abbey and we saw him no more. It was only later that evening, when we were talking together, that we all realized that the man was indeed Ross — but then he could not have been, because we had all been there, the day that he died.'

'Tell me, Mr Ganniford, can you be absolutely certain that the dead man all those years ago was in fact Charles Ross? Could another person have been shot by mistake? The inquest stated that the side of his face was blown away. His features must have been unrecognizable, but you all assumed it was Ross. Perhaps Ross was not there at all that weekend, and that someone else had taken his place?'

'No, it was definitely Ross. Although Jenkins, and myself had never met Ross before that weekend, he was known to Colonel Eames and Anstruther, as they were both members of the regiment. When we came across the body, although the face was gone, we all knew it was Ross, same clothes and stature, there was no doubting it.'

'So who was the man at the abbey if it wasn't Ross?' asked Crabb, looking up from his notebook.

'I don't know, but the more I think about it the more I believe that it was Ross. I cannot understand it; dead men don't return from the grave, do they, Ravenscroft?' said Ganniford, reclaiming his armchair and mopping his sweating brow with a large handkerchief.

'Miss Eames, can you add anything to what Mr Ganniford has just told us?' asked Ravenscroft turning towards the lady.

'I am afraid not, Inspector. I knew nothing of these past affairs until after that night in the abbey.'

'Did your father ever mention to you the events of that weekend?'

'I remember his visit to Lord Treaves, but he said nothing about what had transpired when he returned home.'

'Did your father ever talk about the massacre in Afghanistan?' continued Ravenscroft.

'No. My mother and I were at home in Ludlow when my father was in India with his regiment. He considered that it would be better if we remained in England. When he and his regiment returned home, he spoke very little of his days in India and Afghanistan. He retired some years ago. I am sorry that I cannot help you further.'

'Thank you, Miss Eames. It is a pity, Mr Ganniford, that you and your companions weren't more forthcoming when I first interviewed you all. If we had learned the truth at the start of this investigation, the lives of Major Anstruther and Dr Hollinger might have been saved.'

'You don't know that, man,' retorted an indignant Ganniford. 'You don't know that at all.'

'If you will both excuse me, I must put into operation the search for Mr Jenkins. The sooner he is found, the better it will be for all of us. Come, Crabb. Good day to you both.'

* * *

'If only we had known all about Ross's death, we would not have been led astray by all that nonsense about missing golden goblets,' sighed Ravenscroft, as he sank into his chair in the police station in Tewkesbury.

'That is why they all came here,' said Crabb, taking the other chair.

'Yes. They all believed they were descendants of Sir Roger de la Pole and that if they came to Tewkesbury they would each stand to have a share in the old Templar's treasure once it was retrieved. We now know that Crosbie was merely using the story to bring them all to the town — but why, Tom? What was his purpose in reuniting the members of the hunting party after all these years?'

'And two of them are now dead,' added Crabb.

'Exactly, and we must not forget that there was another victim, Crosbie himself, who was hit over the head and left in the open tomb. Whoever is behind all this must have been in league with Crosbie right from the start, and once Crosbie had performed his role in bringing the members of the hunting party together, he was of no further use to our murderer and disposed of in a cowardly fashion. But why? Why, Tom?'

'Because our murderer wanted to be sure that Crosbie could not talk.'

'Correct. If Crosbie remained alive, his association with the murderer could be revealed at any moment. No, Crosbie had to be put out of the way. Now what we have to ask ourselves, is why did our murderer want to bring all these people together? If he wanted to kill them all, why did he not just kill them all individually in their own homes? That would have been the easy way, and it would not have aroused suspicion. Why concoct this elaborate story to bring them all here to Tewkesbury? It just does not make any sense at all — unless, of course, he still hoped that one of them might be able to solve the code on the side of the tomb.'

'I thought we had discounted that idea, sir.'

'Yes, you're right. I must put all thought of that Templar out of my mind. So, who do you think is behind all this, Tom?'

'Jenkins? Dry old fish. Don't care for him much. You always get the feeling that he knows a lot more than you do, and that he likes you to know it, if you see what I mean.'

'He certainly has the intelligence and knowledge to come up with this story. To him, it could have been some kind of intellectual game — but do people kill just to fulfil some kind of intelligent desire? I don't know, but if he did kill Crosbie, Hollinger and Anstruther, then it would make sense of the fact that he has left the town in a hurry before we can lay our hands on him.'

'Ganniford?' suggested Crabb.

'Ganniford. Yes, Ganniford, always critical and complaining, but I doubt that he would have had the energy or the inclination to commit three murders.'

'Miss Eames?'

'Miss Eames interests me. We know that her father was the colonel of Ross's regiment and that he was present at the hunting party weekend, although the good lady was not there herself. So why bring Miss Eames here to Tewkesbury, if her father was already dead?'

'Perhaps Crosbie intended that Major Eames should have been present, but then he died unexpectedly and his daughter came in his place?' suggested Crabb.

'I think you may well be right, Tom. She said that her father had only recently died. She must have been there when Crosbie called on her father, and after his death decided that she would journey to Tewkesbury to look for the treasure. Our Miss Eames certainly likes to stay in the background, and I must say I was not entirely convinced when she declared that she knew nothing of the events of both the hunting weekend and that massacre in Afghanistan. I think her father must have told her something — but what possible motive can she have to kill Hollinger, Anstruther and Crosbie? Jenkins, Ganniford or Miss Eames? We are, of course, forgetting one thing in all this: our chief suspect, Ross, is still at large. I am convinced that it is Ross who holds the solution to this mystery.'

'But Ross is dead, sir. Ganniford and Lord Treaves both saw the body and confirmed the death,' said Crabb.

'Yes, that would appear to confirm the newspaper report of the inquest. If Ganniford and the others did lure Ross to Lord Treaves's estate that weekend with the intention of killing him to reclaim the honour of the regiment, then they certainly seem to have fulfilled their intention. I think we can safely assume that the man they saw that night at the abbey and when we interviewed at Bredon's Norton was not Ross. And in my experience dead men don't come back from the dead to seek revenge on those who might have done them wrong in their lifetime. You recall what Ganniford said — although the man told them he was Ross, his face was partially obscured by his large hat and we must remember that ten years had elapsed since the shooting. It was also dark that night and the man quickly disappeared from view once inside the abbey. I think someone was impersonating Ross. He clearly wanted the others to believe he was Ross, but why? Why pretend to be a dead man, and why go around killing two members of the former hunting party? We have not got to the bottom of all this yet. We need to do some more research. I want to know a lot more about that massacre in Afghanistan,' said Ravenscroft, quickly rising from his chair.

'How will you do that, sir? It was all such a long time ago.'

'We must contact the regiment direct and see if they can throw any more light on the event. We also need to know more about Ross's family. Where did he originate from? Kirkintilloch, someone said. Right, Tom, you and I need to pay a visit to the telegraph office, then we must resume our search for Jenkins.'

'The men are out looking for him now, sir,' said Crabb following Ravenscroft out of the room.

'Whatever is all that shouting outside?' said Ravenscroft throwing open the outer door of the building.

'Now quieten down, my lad. I've told you Mr Ravenscroft is busy and not to be disturbed,' said a breathless Reynolds seeking to restrain the youthful Stebbins by holding the young servant's collar.

'What is all this about, Reynolds?' enquired Ravenscroft.

'Thank the lord, Mr Ravenscroft! This puffed-up gent who calls himself an officer of the law, won't let me speak to you on a matter of greatest urgency,' said an indignant Stebbins, trying to free himself from the other's grasp.

'Troublemaker if ever I saw one!' proclaimed Reynolds.

'Let go! Yer strangling me, you great bluebottle!'

'All right, Reynolds, you can let the lad go. Now, Stebbins, what's this all about? Be quick, we are on urgent business,' said Ravenscroft, beginning to move away down the street.

'It's that gent, sir,' said a relieved Stebbins, brushing down his uniform as he ran after the policemen.

'Jenkins?' asked Crabb.

'Yes, him. I reckon I knows where he might be.'

'Where, Stebbins, where?' asked Ravenscroft, suddenly stopping and facing the boy.

'Most like he be under the big wheel.'

'What wheel?'

'The big wheel down at the mill on the weir,' replied Stebbins, growing in self-importance.

'You have seen Mr Jenkins there?' asked Ravenscroft looking anxiously at Crabb.

'No, I ain't actually seen him there.'

'I knew he was wasting our time,' nodded Reynolds, expressing a degree of satisfaction.

'Then how do you know Mr Jenkins is there, Stebbins, if you have not actually seen him?' enquired an indignant Ravenscroft.

''Cause that's where they all ends up.'

'Where who ends up?'

'The stiffs, sir. That's where they all ends up — under the big mill wheel by the weir.'

'And how do you know that, Stebbins? I thought you had only been here in Tewkesbury for a few months.'

'Been talking with the other lads, I have. I has been a making a few enquiries on your behalf, Mr Ravenscroft. They says when folk goes missing, they is always found under the big wheel.'

'I'll send him packing, sir,' said Reynolds.

'Could be worth taking a look?' suggested Crabb.

'Now look here, Stebbins, if you have been making all this up—'

'On the good Queen's life, bless her, and the dead Albert,' interrupted the boy, crossing himself.

'Right, then we had better go and see,' said Ravenscroft. 'Just where is this watermill, Reynolds?'

'Not far, sir,' replied the constable with annoyance.

'Then lead on, Reynolds. Stebbins, you had better accompany us.'

'Delighted, Mr Ravenscroft,' said the boy, giving the constable a broad grin.

The party turned away from the main street and followed a smaller road that ran down towards the river.

'That looks like a mill,' said Crabb, pointing at a large building that came presently into view.

'And that, if I am not mistaken, must be the wheel that turns the water away from the weir,' said Ravenscroft.

'Told you so, Mr Ravenscroft. If your mister has met his end in that river, that's where he'll be and no mistake,' announced Stebbins.

'Looks as though someone is here before us, sir,' said Crabb, pointing to a lone figure who was approaching quickly along the river-bank from the other direction.

'Good morning, Reverend,' called out Ravenscroft.

'Good morning to you, Inspector, gentlemen,' replied the Reverend Jesterson. 'It is indeed a pleasant morning for a stroll by the river.'

'Indeed so, Reverend. The noise from the water is quite deafening,' said Ravenscroft drawing nearer.

'Can't see anything, sir,' said Crabb, trying to make himself heard, as the group peered over the edge of the small wall that separated the bank from the revolving wheel.

'Can I ask what it is that you are looking for?' asked Jesterson.

'There he is, Mr Ravenscroft!' shouted Stebbins excitedly, pointing down into the waters.

'Don't be daft, lad,' said Reynolds. 'That's just a sack and some old driftwood.'

'I tells you it's him!' said Stebbins, leaning so far forward that Crabb felt compelled to restrain the eager young man by grasping the collar of his coat.

'I think he might just be right. Run and get that pole on the side of the bank, Crabb,' instructed Ravenscroft, straining for a better view.

'Whatever is the matter?' asked an anxious Jesterson.

'It's him, the one with the long nose. Dead as last year's cold cucumber if you asks me,' proclaimed Stebbins.

'We don't know that just yet, Stebbins. Here, give me the pole, Crabb, and I will try and hook whatever it is,' said Ravenscroft. 'Here we are. Help me pull it into the side. Good God! The boy is right. It is a body!'

CHAPTER ELEVEN

TEWKESBURY

Ravenscroft looked at the blank wall before him. Two hours before he and Crabb had taken the body recovered from beneath the mill wheel to the local mortuary, where an examination had shown that the deceased had died as the result of a blow to the back of the head. Whether the blow was inflicted before the body was thrown into the waters of the Severn, or whether death was caused as the result of the unfortunate victim falling into the river and then hitting his head on a large stone or the mill wheel, was uncertain. Either way, Jenkins was now dead, and another suspect had ceased to be. Just how Jenkins had found his way to the river when the abbey was in the opposite direction when he had left the Hop Pole earlier that morning, remained a mystery. There was no way that Ravenscroft could prove whether the dead man had died as the result of an accident or had been cruelly struck down by another.

First Hollinger, then Anstruther — and now Jenkins. Now there only remained Ganniford and Miss Eames of the original six members of the group, and, of course, the mysterious, elusive Ross. Ravenscroft was convinced that the

Scotsman was behind all the killings, and that they had something to do with that massacre in Afghanistan and Ross's 'supposed' death at Lord Treaves's weekend gathering, but the more he considered the matter, the more difficult it became to understand why a dead man would come back from the grave to seek revenge on the members of that hunting party.

The door suddenly opened and Tom Crabb entered the room.

'Well, Tom, any news yet?' asked Ravenscroft, quickly removing his feet from the table in front of him.

'None sir.'

'Confound it. We must half the county looking for this fellow Ross, and yet no one has seen him. He can't just have gone to ground. Any replies yet from the telegrams we sent out?'

'Not yet. I've told the boy to bring us any reply as soon as it is received.'

'I can't stand all this waiting around, Tom. There must be something else we can do,' said Ravenscroft, standing up and pacing the room.

'Have you considered the possibility that Jenkins might have thrown himself into the river?' suggested Crabb, unable to think of anything else that might relieve his superior's anxiety.

'You mean that Jenkins was so full of remorse after killing Anstruther and Hollinger that he decided to do away with himself? I don't think so.'

'Just a thought,' said Crabb turning away.

'He didn't seem to be the type who would do that. Talking of Jenkins, how did you think Ganniford and Miss Eames took the news?'

'Ganniford seemed very upset. I suppose they had been friends for many years.'

'And Miss Eames?'

'How do you mean? She sat there and said nothing.'

'That was just it. I thought she might have broken down, but, no, she merely turned away and sat quietly in her chair.'

'Probably the shock was too much for her.'

'No doubt you are right.'

'Have you considered the possibility that Jesterson might be behind all this?' suggested Crabb.

'Go on.'

'Well, it seems just more than a coincidence that he was walking along the river-bank when we arrived at the mill.'

'You think he might have just killed Jenkins?'

'He could have done. We only have his word for it that Jenkins hadn't visited the abbey shortly before his death. Then he was there that night outside the Hop Pole when Anstruther left just after Hollinger's murder. It could be just another coincidence. Can't say I like the gentleman. Something about him doesn't seem right.'

'I still can't see Jesterson as our killer, or even working in conjunction with someone else. What reason would he have for killing Hollinger, Anstruther and Jenkins?'

'Just an idea,' said a crestfallen Crabb.

'Damn it. What are we missing, Tom? There has to be something else; something which we have overlooked. Why, yes of course — the Army List!' said Ravenscroft suddenly stopping in the centre of the room.

'I'm sorry?'

'The Army List! You remember when I sent you to the local library the other day to look up Major Anstruther in the Army List, and you couldn't find him there. That must have been because he had left his regiment some years previously but he still wanted us to believe that he was with the Guards. Did you look up Ross?'

'No, sir,' replied a baffled Crabb. 'At that time we knew nothing of Ross.'

'Exactly! Tell me, Tom, did the library have back copies of the Army List for previous years?' asked Ravenscroft eagerly.

'I believe so, sir, although it was difficult to tell, as the books were all over the place.'

'Then let us go and consult them. Tell Reynolds to bring any telegrams that might arrive to us there as soon as possible.'

* * *

'Good morning to you, Mr Webster,' said Ravenscroft smiling, as he and Crabb entered the library a few minutes later.

The librarian looked up from his work, and gave the men a far from encouraging look of recognition. 'Mr Ravenscroft, it is you again.'

'It is indeed.'

'Pray, sir, how do you know my name? I thought I had not told it you on your previous visit. No, I did not.'

'You are correct, sir — but then there is a well-worn plaque attached to the outside of these premises which informs one, albeit it in rather faded letters, that one might find a librarian by the name of Webster inside this building.'

The librarian's mouth gave a slight twitch as he resumed his work.

'It is back copies of the Army List that my assistant and I need to consult.'

'The Army List, you say? That is a very unusual thing to request, if I may say so. A very unusual request indeed. Yes it is. I do not know where such an item, or items may be found. No, I do not.'

'Crabb, where did you find the volume when you visited the other day?' sighed Ravenscroft.

'On the shelf over here, sir,' replied Crabb, leading the way.

'That may be the wrong part of the library, gentlemen, in which to seek such an item. Then again you may be correct, and you may well find that which you are seeking. I cannot say. No, I cannot say so at all with any great degree of certainty,' began the librarian, quickly rising from his seat.

'Here we are, sir. This was the present volume. These look like some earlier volumes,' said Crabb, reaching up to one of the shelves.

'Fortunately the run would appear to go back a number of years. 1877, let's start with that one,' said Ravenscroft, opening one of the small, leather-bound volumes and turning over the pages. 'Ah, here we are: Captain Charles Ross, formerly of Kirkintilloch, Dumbartonshire, Scotland. Try the next one, 1878, Tom, whilst I look in 1879.'

'I see you are fruitful in your search, gentlemen. That is good. Yes, it is, indeed.'

The two men ignored the librarian as they eagerly continued with their research.

'Yes, here he is again, sir,' said Tom looking up from the volume.

'So he was still listed in 1878. That was when the incident in Afghanistan must have taken place. He is still listed here for 1879, although he must have left the army by then, but the list was probably several months out of date when it was published. Let us try 1880. Ah, here we are, see there is no entry for Captain Charles Ross for that year.'

'Not surprising, sir, as he was dead by then,' said Crabb, still puzzled by his superior's line of new enquiry.

'Take the other volumes. Start with 1881.'

'I don't understand.'

'Humour me, Crabb. 1882 nothing there. Try 1883. No, nothing,' said Ravenscroft, quickly turning over the pages of the volumes.

'1884. Nothing for Ross here,' said Crabb.

'Damn! I was convinced that— 1885. Look here, Crabb! Captain Robert Ross. Formerly of Kirkintilloch.'

'Robert Ross?'

'Yes — and see here, 1886. The same entry. Try the next one, while I take a look for 1888,' instructed Ravenscroft.

'Yes, sir. 1887. Captain Robert Ross,' said Crabb.

'But there is no entry for 1888. Do you see what this means, Tom? Captain Robert Ross of Kirkintilloch was serving in the army from 1885 until 1887. The fact that he is not listed in 1888, last year's volume, suggests that he had left the army by then,' said Ravenscroft excitedly.

'I still don't understand, sir.'

'Robert Ross was related to our Charles Ross — possibly a younger brother — and both came from Kirkintilloch!'

'So Charles Ross did die at that hunting party after all.'

'Exactly! And the man we saw at Bredon's Norton was not Charles Ross but his brother Robert — and have you noticed something else, Crabb? They are both listed as serving in the same regiment in India and Afghanistan!'

* * *

'You think that Robert Ross killed Anstruther, Hollinger and Jenkins because he believed that they had shot his brother?' asked Crabb, as he and Ravenscroft made their way back to the station.

'I am certain of it. He used Crosbie to lure those whom he felt responsible for his brother's death, on the pretext that they were all entitled to a share of the old knight's treasure. He knew that they would all be more than anxious not to miss out on the opportunity,' replied Ravenscroft.

'Very clever.'

'And once Crosbie had performed his role he was disposable.'

'Why didn't Ross just eliminate them one by one in their own homes?'

'Perhaps he derived some kind of pleasure or satisfaction in watching how the others would react, one by one, as they learned of the others' deaths. What I don't understand is, why? Why would Robert Ross seek revenge for his brother's death, when Charles Ross had bought dishonour and shame on his family due to his cowardice in Afghanistan? You would think that Ross would have wanted nothing to do with his brother's memory after that act of cowardice. No, I cannot see that he would act out of revenge.'

'Here is Reynolds, sir,' interrupted Crabb.

'Ah, Reynolds, I trust you have news for me,' said Ravenscroft as the policeman drew near.

'Yes, sir. Telegram just arrived,' replied the constable passing over the item to his superior.

'Thank you, Reynolds,' said Ravenscroft eagerly, tearing open the envelope. 'It's from the colonel of Ross's old regiment. *Can confirm massacre took place. Ross discredited at time. New evidence suggests however that Ross fought with honour.*'

'What does that mean, "fought with honour"?' asked Crabb.

'It means that Charles Ross did not desert his post that day. He must have fought bravely to save the others and was wrongly accused of cowardice at the time. If Anstruther and the others did shoot Ross during the hunting party, they must have believed at the time that Charles Ross was guilty of cowardice and that they were acting to restore the honour of the regiment. If Robert Ross joined the regiment some years later, and somehow learned of what really happened at that massacre, then he must have believed that his brother had been unjustly treated — and somehow wanted revenge on those who had caused his brother's death!' exclaimed Ravenscroft.

'So that is why Ross killed Anstruther and the others?'

'My God, Crabb! We have been so stupid. Do you see what this means?'

'What, sir?'

'It means that even as we speak, Ganniford and Miss Eames are in the gravest danger!'

* * *

Ravenscroft ran into the Hop Pole, closely followed by Crabb and Reynolds.

'Lord, Mr Ravenscroft, you is in a mighty hurry,' said Stebbins, looking up from the desk in the reception area. 'Somat must be up.'

'Where are Mr Ganniford and Miss Eames?' asked Ravenscroft urgently.

'Last seen in the snug, sir,' answered the boy.

Ravenscroft quickly made his way across the bar and into the snug. 'Thank goodness,' he remarked, as Ganniford came forward to meet them.

'Whatever is the matter, Inspector?' asked Ganniford taken aback by the sudden intrusion.

'I believe that you and Miss Eames are in the gravest danger.'

'From Ross?'

'From Ross. There is no time to explain now. Where is Miss Eames?' asked Ravenscroft looking anxiously around the room.

'She said she was going out for a walk,' answered Ganniford.

'And you let her go alone?' retorted Ravenscroft.

'I could see no harm in it. The good lady said she wanted to be alone.'

'How long ago was this?'

'About five minutes ago.'

'We are too late!' exclaimed Ravenscroft. 'Quickly, man, can you remember where Miss Eames said she might be taking her walk?'

'Into the town I believe, or was it down by the river? Blessed if I can remember,' said a confused Ganniford scratching his head.

'It is very important that you do remember, Mr Ganniford. I believe that Miss Eames is in the gravest danger,' implored Ravenscroft.

'Yes, yes, I remember. She said she was going to take a walk around the abbey grounds. Yes, that was it, the abbey grounds.'

'Quickly, Crabb. We must make all speed,' said Ravenscroft, rushing out of the room.

The two men made their way out of the inn and ran quickly across the road, followed by Reynolds, Ganniford and an eager Stebbins.

'Which way, sir?' asked Crabb, pausing at the entrance to the abbey grounds.

'This way I would think,' replied Ravenscroft, turning towards the right.

The group followed Ravenscroft across the lawns that ran in front and to the side of the abbey.

'Over there!' shouted Crabb, pointing towards a distant figure.

'Thank God we are in time to save the good lady,' said Ravenscroft quickening his pace. 'Who is that black-coated figure moving towards her?'

'It's Ross, sir!' exclaimed Crabb.

'We must save her!' replied Ravenscroft.

'He has her, sir!' said Crabb.

As the group drew nearer to the couple, Ravenscroft observed that Ross had grabbed his quarry.

'Leave her alone!' shouted a breathless Ravenscroft, drawing closer to the couple.

Ross turned to face Ravenscroft, one arm around Miss Eames's waist, the other clasping a knife to her throat.

'It's finished, Ross. Let Miss Eames go,' commanded Ravenscroft, as the remainder of his party came running up behind him.

'Keep back, Ravenscroft, or I'll kill the lady,' shouted Ross. 'Tell them all to keep back! I mean what I say.'

Miss Eames attempted to let out a cry as she struggled to free herself from her assailant's grasp.

'It's all over, Ross. We know what really happened in Afghanistan,' replied Ravenscroft, raising his arm to indicate that Crabb and the others were to stand back.

'You know nothing!' sneered Ross.

'We know that your brother was unjustly vilified.'

'Then you know why I have to avenge his death.'

'Your brother died as the result of a hunting accident,' said Ganniford.

'Lies! Lies! You, Ganniford, and the rest of them killed him!'

'I swear it was an accident. His gun discharged itself. We had nothing to do with it,' said an agitated Ganniford.

'Lies! Lies! You miserable man.'

'Let Miss Eames go,' said Ravenscroft, observing that Crabb and Reynolds had slowly moved out to his right and left sides. 'She has done your family no harm. She was not even there that weekend.'

'She is the daughter of Colonel Eames and will die in his place,' retorted Ross tightening his grip on the struggling lady and drawing the knife nearer to her throat.

'For goodness' sake, man, you know it is all over. Let Miss Eames go. You can't take all five of us. We are too many for you.'

Ross looked frantically from side to side. 'Tell them to keep back!' he yelled.

'It's all finished, man. Give me the knife,' instructed Ravenscroft taking a step forward.

'I warn you, Ravenscroft, keep back all of you,' shouted Ross.

'Let me have a go at him!' shouted Stebbins, suddenly running towards the couple.

'Stebbins! Keep back!' yelled Ravenscroft.

As the boy dived for Ross's legs, Miss Eames suddenly broke free, and Crabb and Reynolds ran in and quickly wrestled the man to the ground.

'Put the cuffs on him, Crabb. You silly boy, you could have had Miss Eames killed,' said Ravenscroft reprimanding Stebbins.

A sobbing Miss Eames ran into Ganniford's arms.

'Always go for the legs, my old dad used to say. The legs, my boy, that's where they least expect it.'

'One of these days, Stebbins, your impetuosity will lead you to meet an untimely end.'

'Not yet though eh, Mr Ravenscroft?' smiled a triumphant Stebbins.

'What shall we do with him, sir?' enquired Reynolds, as he and Crabb raised a defeated Ross to his feet.

'Confound you, Ravenscroft,' muttered a dishevelled Ross.

'So, Mr Ross, we have you at last. Take him to the station, Crabb. I will deal with him later.'

CHAPTER TWELVE

TEWKESBURY

Ravenscroft entered the room. Ross, seated at the table, turned and stared out of the window, his face expressionless.

'Well, Mr Ross, what have you to say for yourself?' asked Ravenscroft drawing up the other chair, while Crabb moved to the corner of the room and took out his notebook.

His prisoner said nothing.

'Silence will do you no good, Mr Ross. I need to hear your side of the story.'

'Story! This is not a story,' snapped Ross, turning suddenly in Ravenscroft's direction and thumping his fist hard down on the table. 'The honour of my family has been tainted. Don't you understand that?'

'Then why do you not try and explain it to me, Mr Ross?'

'You would not understand. There is no point,' said Ross, slumping back in the chair.

'I know that the deaths of four men lie at your door,' retorted Ravenscroft, regretting the words of provocation as soon as he had spoken them.

'My brother was a good man. I grew up admiring him for his courage, his bravery and his honour. I worshipped the very ground that he stood on. He was everything to me, don't you understand? All I wanted to do, Ravenscroft, was to join his regiment when I came of age, so that I could prove myself half the man he was.'

'Go on,' urged Ravenscroft.

'The regiment went to India. Then we heard about that terrible massacre by those murdering Afghans. Over fifty men, women and children were slaughtered that day. Do you know that they even cut off the children's heads and stuck them on pikes? Some of them were as young as three. What kind of man does that? What they did to the women was even worse. Unspeakable! And my brother was the only one to survive. They said that he had deserted his post, had left all the others to be butchered. Can you imagine the disgrace, Ravenscroft? Our friends in society would not speak to us. People spat at us when we crossed the street. When Charles returned home, after he had been thrown out the army, my father and mother would have nothing to do with him, so Charles left the home where he had been born and raised. We heard later that he had purchased a house near Bredon. God knows why he went there. He just wanted to be alone, I suppose; to escape from everyone and everything.

'Then we heard that he had been killed at a shooting party. I shed no tears. Perhaps he had done the honourable thing in the end — taken the easy way out and shot himself. My dear mother who had never hurt anyone in her life, died of a broken heart. Her dying wish was that I should join the regiment and restore the family honour. So that is what I did, and for three years I went to fight in India — but do you know something, my fellow officers hated and despised me. They said I came from a coward's family; that my brother had bought dishonour and disgrace to the regiment, and that I would pay for his actions. For three years I had to endure their insults and mockery. Do you know what that felt like? To be treated like an outcast, to be given the foulest of food, to be sent on the worst of engagements, to be sneered at and humiliated. And, worst of all, I did not complain. Never once did I complain. It was, after all, my penance. I had to suffer for the disgrace that my brother had bought on us all. I'm sorry, can I have some water?' gasped Ross, tears of anger beginning to form in his eyes.

'Of course. Crabb, bring the prisoner a glass of water, if you will,' instructed Ravenscroft.

The two men sat in silence until Crabb returned to the room bearing a jug of water. Ravenscroft poured out some of the liquid into a glass. Ross seized it and gulped it down.

'When you are ready to continue,' said Ravenscroft, leaning back in his chair once more.

'One evening, Major Anstruther, who was in our regiment, became the worse for drink, boasted how he and the others — Ganniford, Jenkins, Hollinger and Colonel Eames, had persuaded Lord Treaves to invite my brother to his estate for the weekend, and how they cornered him in that field and confronted him with his cowardice. Anstruther laughed when he told how they had forced my brother to kneel before them and beg for his own life, how they had mocked him and humiliated him and then shot him, and how they all swore an oath to make the whole thing look like an accident. And do you know, Ravenscroft, when I heard that man bragging and boasting in his intoxicated state, I kind of admired him? At least he and the others had done something to avenge the deaths of all those innocent men, women and children. After all, my brother had betrayed them all in order to save his own skin,' said Ross, becoming increasingly animated and staring round the room with a look of wide-eyed desperation.

Ravenscroft replenished his prisoner's glass, then looked across at Crabb who was busily engaged in taking notes.

'Then one day everything changed. I came across an old Sikh, who wandered into the garrison. He had heard that a soldier of the name of Ross was there and asked to speak with him. When I approached the man, however, he said that I was not Captain Ross. I explained to him that I was his brother, and that Charles was dead. Then he told me what had really happened on that day. He had seen it all — how the party had been ambushed in the hills by the Afghans — how my brother had quickly organized the defence, killing many of the attackers as he did so, fighting bravely in a futile attempt to save the lives of the others, until he received a blow on the back of his head and was knocked unconscious. They must have thought they had killed him and left him for dead. How Charles survived the slaughter I do not know. When the murdering cutthroats had left, the old Sikh, who had been observing events from behind a rock, scoured the battlefield for survivors, where he found my brother still alive, but badly injured, and took him back to his own village where the people of his tribe cared for him. It was some weeks before my brother was fit enough to leave and return to his regiment — but, of course, news of the massacre had spread by then, and everyone in the regiment had assumed that Charles had deserted his post. There was no one who could confirm what had really happened, and despite his attempts to assert his own innocence in the affair, he was entirely discredited and forced out of the army. So you see, Ravenscroft, my brother was never the coward they all said he was. He had fought with honour and with bravery.'

Ross paused from his narrative and reached out again for the water and bought the glass to his lips with trembling hands.

'God, how they had all chosen to disbelieve him! Eames and Anstruther had already left the regiment and returned home before I learned the truth. Once the old man had told everyone the true account of what had really happened that day, the new colonel of the regiment restored my brother's honour — but by then it was all too late, he had been killed by Anstruther and the others all those years before. Both my parents had died believing that their son had bought dishonour to the family, when in fact the opposite was the case. Worst of all, I had joined in the condemnation, believing in my brother's betrayal.'

'What did you do next?' asked Ravenscroft intently.

'I resigned my commission and returned home. I did not know what else I could do to restore my brother's honour.

People in Kirkintilloch still believed in Charles's guilt. So, I decided to move to Bredon's Norton where I knew that Charles had purchased a house and some land shortly before his death. There I tried to put the past behind me, but however much I tried, I could not. Somehow I had betrayed my brother by my own condemnation. It was as if I had been there that day when he had been shot. Then I became angry when I remembered the words of Anstruther and how he and the others had humiliated and degraded my brother before they had killed him in such a brutal fashion, and I knew that the honour of my brother and my family could only be restored by the deaths of those men who had bought about Charles's death. At first I thought it would be a simple matter just to kill them all one at a time, but then I realized that would be far too easy. I wanted them each to know the fear and terror as their companions were killed one by one, wondering when it would be their turn to pay for the death of my brother!'

'I think I can understand that,' said Ravenscroft, knowing that he would need to offer some words of encouragement so that the full confession could be obtained.

'You have no idea how I felt; how the anger increased inside me; how all I wanted was revenge on those who had killed my brother. But how was I to bring all these people together? Then I learned of the legend of Sir Roger de la Pole here in the abbey and of the treasure he had bought back with him from the Holy Land, and I saw a way in which they could all be reunited. So I engaged the services of an old school friend of mine.'

'Crosbie,' interjected Ravenscroft.

'You know him by that name. He had fallen on hard times. His employer, a lawyer, had recently died and he was without employment. I outlined my plan to him — how we would bring the six of them here to Tewkesbury and use them to discover the hiding place of the old Templar's treasure. Of course, I did not tell him my true intentions. So, I compiled the chart, showing how each of them was descended from Sir Roger de la Pole and Crosbie began his work visiting each of them in turn and baiting the trap. We were careful that Crosbie chose a new name for each person he visited.'

'The novels of Anthony Trollope,' added Ravenscroft.

'Ah, you spotted that.'

'It was my wife who saw the connection.'

'And so they all came that night here to Tewkesbury lured by greed and expectation, swarming like bees round a honey pot. I had told them to meet each other outside the abbey at midnight. At first I knew that they would not recognize me in the dark, and with my face partially concealed, but I knew that it would not take them long to realize that Charles Ross had returned from the grave,' laughed Ross slumping backwards in his chair.

'Why did you then kill Crosbie?' asked Ravenscroft.

'He had performed his role well. Earlier that evening we had entered the abbey and had together prised open the lid of the coffin. If there was any treasure to be found, then we might as well acquire it for ourselves. I encouraged Crosbie to climb inside the sarcophagus, but there was only a few bones. It was then that I killed him. You see, I could not afford to let him go. He knew too much and might betray me before my plan could be carried out. Then I tried to pull the cover back on the coffin, but it was too heavy for me to move alone. I realized that it would be interesting if I left things the way they were, so that the others would feel uneasy upon finding the dead man inside the coffin, and would begin to wonder why the man who had been instrumental in bringing them there was now dead. When I met the others later, I quickly slipped into the darkness and watched as they found his body inside the tomb. When your constable arrived and confronted them, I took the opportunity to leave the abbey unseen by anyone. I watched as you arrived the next day and began your questioning, but I knew that none of them would tell you the real reason for their visit here.'

'How did you come to kill Hollinger?'

'I decided that my first victim would be Hollinger. Shortly after he retired I crept into his room and killed him. It was so easy. He was just lying there. He did not even hear me enter the room. I decided that Anstuther would also die that night, but when I went to his room, I found that he had already left. The man had always been a coward. Perhaps he had realized that his life was in danger and had decided to leave before I could extract my revenge. It looked as though my plan would be thwarted, but then I decided that if I left my bloodstained clothes in his room it would look as though he had committed the murder, and you would do everything in your power to look for him and bring him back here. When your officers brought him back and you began your questioning, I knew that I would have to act quickly. I couldn't risk Anstruther telling you about the killing of my brother, so when you were away and your constable was taking him his food, I slipped into the front office with the poisoned drink, making sure that no one saw me. It was all so ridiculously easy. I was only sorry that I was not there in person to see him die. The man had been a braggart and waster all his life!'

Ravenscroft poured out more water for his prisoner.

'I knew now that the others would know that I had killed their companions — but I was also confident that they would never tell you about that weekend when my brother had been shot. If they had told you the truth they would have had to admit their own part in his murder.'

'How did you kill Jenkins?' asked Ravenscroft.

'That was easy. I knew that all I had to do was to wait for the right opportunity when one of them would be alone. When Jenkins left the inn, I made sure that he saw me walking down towards the river. I knew that his curiosity would get the better of him. All I had to do was wait for him to reach the river, creep up behind him and strike the back of his head, before throwing him over the weir.'

'And poor Miss Eames would have been your next victim?'

'Yes, but then, of course, you had at last unravelled the truth. The rest you know. Do you know something, Ravenscroft? I am glad that I managed to kill Hollinger, Anstruther and Jenkins. They deserved to die for their part in my brother's death and for the blackening of my families name. My only regret is that I was not able to kill that wind-bag Ganniford and that insipid Eames woman. I feel that I have only partly avenged my brother!'

'Miss Eames played no part in your brother's death,' said Ravenscroft, observing that his prisoner had begun shaking uncontrollably.

'Eames was dead, it was only right that his daughter should stand in his place!' snapped Ross.

'Good God, man, do you have no remorse? You are responsible for the deaths of four men,' retorted Ravenscroft.

'Remorse! You say that I should show some regret for my actions? What pity did they show to my brother when they cornered him in that field?' replied Ross, burying his face in his hands. 'Charles fought with honour and with gallantry to save the lives of those men, women and children, but he was branded a coward and killed in a brutal cowardly fashion! Surely you can see that? What will happen to me, now?'

'You will face trial for the deaths of Crosbie, Hollinger, Anstruther and Jenkins — and you will almost certainly hang,' said Ravenscroft with contempt, rising from his seat and indicating that the interview was at an end.

Ross let out a loud laugh and reached into his pocket.

'Take him back to his cell, Crabb,' instructed Ravenscroft, beginning to leave the room.

'Quickly, sir!' shouted Crabb.

Ross poured some liquid into his glass and, throwing back his head, drained it, before Ravenscroft could wrestle the container from his grasp.

'You are too late, Ravenscroft!' laughed Ross.

'No. Good God, man, not this way!' said Ravenscroft, unable to do anything as Ross's body shook violently before collapsing in the chair.

'He must have had the poison on his person,' said a startled Crabb standing back from the corpse.

'Damn the man! He has escaped the hangman's noose!'

* * *

'Well Mr Ravenscroft, if you have no further need of us, Miss Eames and I with leave you,' said Ganniford standing outside the Hop Pole later that day.

'Yes, everything is in order. I have your statements. Everything is at an end,' replied Ravenscroft.

'I am only sorry that my poor friend Jenkins will not be leaving with us. I will miss our talks together. He was a good man, you know. He did not deserve to die like that. However Miss Eames has agreed to accompany me to London, where I will be pleased to offer her my protection,' said Ganniford kissing his companion's hand before stepping into the cab.

'Good day to you, Miss Eames,' said Ravenscroft nodding in the lady's direction.

'Good day to you, Inspector,' smiled Miss Eames. 'Perhaps we will meet again one day.'

'Right then, Ravenscroft. Jolly well done and all that. We caught that murdering scoundrel in the end,' said Ganniford as the cabman urged the horse forward.

Ravenscroft and Crabb watched as the vehicle turned the corner.

'We should have arrested him for the murder of Charles Ross,' muttered Crabb.

'It would do no good. No jury would convict him on the evidence now that Robert Ross himself is dead. Ganniford would deny everything, no doubt still maintaining that Charles Ross shot himself as the result of an accident. No, the events of the past have cast a long and deep shadow over the lives of too many people. Let Ganniford and Miss Eames make something of their lives if they can.'

'I suppose you're right, sir.'

'There is one question that we will never know the answer to.'

'Oh, what's that?' asked Crabb.

'Why that poor Crosbie fellow only cut the nails on one of his feet, and not the other.'

'What now then, sir?'

'It seems we have been granted permission to open that old tomb in Meysey Hampton. The vicar expects us there next Tuesday at three in the afternoon. There may be treasure to be found after all.'

'You'll be leaving us then, Mr Ravenscroft,' said a grinning Stebbins, emerging from the Hop Pole.

'Yes, Stebbins. We have spent far too long in this town. Our business is all concluded.'

'Took his own life in the end, I hear.'

'That is no concern of yours, Stebbins,' said Ravenscroft mounting his trap.

'Good day to you then, Mr Ravenscroft.'

'Good day to you, Stebbins.'

'Till the next time then. You knows you can call on me at any time. Stebbins is your man.'

'And Stebbins—'

'Yes?'

'Just try and stay out of trouble.'

'I will do my best, sir. Stebbins will do his best.'

* * *

'I must say, my dear, that I am mighty relieved that the case has come to a conclusion. It was not the ending I would have wanted, but I suppose justice has been done in the end.'

Ravenscroft had returned home later that evening and, as they sat before the fire, he had related the events of the day.

'It is quite horrible, to have taken his own life like that and in such an awful fashion,' replied Lucy.

'I would have preferred it if we had bought him to trial, but he was too quick for us.'

'One can almost feel sorry for the poor man, after the dreadful way both he and his brother had been treated, when all the time his brother had done everything possible to save the lives of those innocent women and children. How terrible it must have been. I can think of nothing more horrible than to be killed in such a terrible place. I suppose that is where all this began, one day in a strange land, all those years ago.'

'Let us not forget the lives of the four people he took whilst carrying out his plan of revenge. Nothing can justify the taking of another life, whether innocent or guilty. There is no excuse for cold-blooded murder. Revenge can often affect a man's reason.'

'Do you think that Anstruther and the others did kill Ross's brother at that shooting party — or was it just an accident as the papers and your Mr Ganniford claimed?' asked Lucy looking up from her sewing.

'I have no way of telling. The truth of the matter may never be revealed. Most of the members of that shooting party are now dead. Lord Treaves was not at the actual shoot, so we only have Ganniford's word that it was an accident.'

'I suppose so, but what an ingenious plan, to bring all the people he hated to Tewkesbury, using the story of the Templar Knight and his long lost treasure to bring them there.'

'And enrolling the services of his friend Crosbie to make them believe that the treasure was there for the taking. I suppose he could not resist the use of all those names. It was very clever of you, my dear, to have spotted that,' said Ravenscroft, stirring the embers of the fire with the poker.

'Samuel, can I ask you something?' asked Lucy after a moment's silence had elapsed.

'Yes, my dear, of course.'

'I hope you will not object.'

'How could I refuse you anything?'

'Well, you know that you are going to Meysey Hampton next Tuesday, now that you have been granted permission by the bishop to open that tomb. I should so like to go with you. It all sounds rather exciting.'

'Of course you shall come with me. How can I deny you? I must say that I am rather looking forward to the occasion. It was Salt who finally solved the puzzle of the inscription on the side of the tomb after all these centuries, thus enabling Tom and I to visit the village of Meysey Hampton, where we were fortunate enough to find the old tomb with the inscription above it. Let us hope that we can now finally reveal the secret of Sir Roger de la Pole.'

CHAPTER THIRTEEN

SIR ROGER'S SECRET REVEALED

A few days later, Ravenscroft and Lucy found themselves walking up the pathway towards the front entrance of the church in the village of Meysey Hampton.

'What a beautiful village,' remarked Lucy. 'It would be nice to live in such a place.'

'I thought you were content to reside in Ledbury,' replied Ravenscroft.

'Good morning to you, sir, and Mrs Ravenscroft,' said a smiling Tom Crabb emerging from the porchway of the church.

'Good morning to you, Tom. I trust everything is ready for the opening of the tomb?'

'Yes, sir. The clergyman is waiting for us inside the building.'

'I wonder what we will find inside the tomb?' asked Lucy.

'Whatever it was, the old Templar thought it to be of sufficient value to have left such baffling instructions to be carved on the outside of his tomb in Tewkesbury after his death.'

'I wonder if he ever thought that one day someone would work out the answer,' said Lucy.

'I think he rather hoped that someone would. After all, why go to that trouble to construct a mystery if you did not want it to be solved at some later date? Clearly whatever he was hiding was of great value to him,' replied Ravenscroft.

'After you, Mrs Ravenscroft, and you, sir,' said Tom opening the door of the church.

Ravenscroft led the way into the church and made his way up the nave followed by the others.

'Mr Ravenscroft,' said the clergyman, coming forward to meet them.

'Reverend,' said Ravenscroft shaking the other's hand. 'May I introduce you to my wife, Mrs Ravenscroft. Constable Crabb you know already. I trust you have no objection to Mrs Ravenscroft being present?'

'None at all. You are most welcome, my dear lady.'

'That is very kind,' replied Lucy, smiling.

'It is very important that there are witnesses who can observe such an occasion. After all, it is not every day that one opens a tomb that has remained sealed for centuries. I must confess to being somewhat apprehensive as to what we might find enclosed within,' said Anson.

'Perhaps we should begin?' suggested Ravenscroft.

'This way, gentlemen, and lady,' said the clergyman, walking over to the old stone sarcophagus.

'Crabb, if you would oblige us by beginning with the hammer and chisel?' instructed Ravenscroft.

'Right, sir,' said Crabb, removing his coat and placing the edge of the chisel at the edge of the covering of the tomb.

Ravenscroft and the others watched as Crabb struck the chisel with the hammer and gradually drove the edge of the tool further into the small gap he had made.

Lucy gently squeezed her husband's arm.

'I think that will do, Crabb,' said Ravenscroft, after a few moments had passed. 'Reverend, perhaps you will be kind enough to assist Constable Crabb and myself in attempting to slide the lid across?'

'Certainly, Inspector.'

Ravenscroft, Crabb and Anson struggled to inch the covering slowly across the top of the tomb, as an anxious Lucy stood watching.

'I think that should enable us to see inside the grave. If we push any more the lid may slide off completely and we will have the deuce of a job to lift it up again and replace it,' said Ravenscroft. 'Stand back, gentlemen — let in some light so that I can see what there is inside.'

'What can you see, my dear sir?' enquired the clergyman wiping his brow.

'There seems to be something here,' said Ravenscroft leaning forward and extending his arm into the tomb. 'Ah, I have it!'

Lucy, Crabb and Anson edged forward.

'A box!' exclaimed Anson.

'Indeed. A simple, plain wooden box,' replied Ravenscroft examining the recovered item.

'Nothing else, sir?' enquired Crabb looking somewhat crestfallen.

'No. The tomb appears to be completely empty, except for this box.'

'It is rather small,' said Lucy, disappointed.

'Yes. I would say it cannot be more than four inches in length.'

'Hardly large enough to contain a golden goblet,' added Crabb.

'I think the lid may lift,' announced Ravenscroft, placing the box on top of the tomb. 'There may be something inside.'

The others eagerly crowded round as Ravenscroft prised open the lid.

'What is it?' asked Crabb.

'It seems to be an old leather bag. Curiouser and curiouser. Just an old bag,' said Ravenscroft.

'What an extraordinary thing to bury inside a tomb,' said a perplexed Anson.

'I believe there may be something inside it,' declared Ravenscroft.

'Perhaps there is some treasure after all,' said a hopeful Crabb.

Ravenscroft tipped the contents of the bag into his hand.

'Sand!' exclaimed Anson. 'A handful of sand!'

'Sand! Where is the sense in that?' said a puzzled Crabb.

'Why bury a handful of sand?' asked Lucy.

'It appears then, my friends, that we have no treasure,' said the clergyman shaking his head.

'How extraordinary,' added Lucy, shaking her head.

'Why go to all that trouble, creating that code on the side of his tomb in the abbey in Tewkesbury, to lead us here to another tomb, which contains only an old leather bag full of sand? It just don't make any sense,' said Crabb.

'A mystery indeed,' remarked Anson.

Ravenscroft remained deep in thought.

'It looks as though your Sir Roger de la Pole had a sense of humour,' suggested Lucy.

'No, I think it is more than that. I believe that Sir Roger had indeed believed that he brought back gold from the Holy Land — but instead of the gold of a precious relic, he brought back something which he considered to be of a far greater value,' said Ravenscroft.

'I don't understand you, sir,' said Crabb.

'He brought back some of the golden sand from a land which had borne witness to the great events of Christendom — sand which Christ himself may well have trodden on. To the old crusader that was treasure indeed.'

* * *

A few minutes later, Ravenscroft and Lucy made their way down the pathway of the churchyard towards the waiting trap.

'So, there you have it, my dear,' said Ravenscroft. 'I hope you were not too disappointed.'

'It would have been nice if the tomb had contained a golden chalice or something of a similar nature, but I can understand why your Sir Roger valued the sand above all other.'

'Yes, the old knight had travelled far and wide, and when he left the Holy Land he chose not the material wealth of gold and precious stones to take away with him, but a simple handful of sand. That was wealth enough for him, and he was ensuring that his gift would be passed down to any future crusader knight who one day might decipher the inscription on his tomb. Anyway, the case is now closed. I think we can now leave Sir Roger in peace inside his tomb in Tewkesbury. At least no one else will want to disturb his bones in the future. Now, my dear, I have something of a surprise for you,' announced Ravenscroft.

'And I also have a surprise for you, Samuel,' said Lucy, linking her arm with that of her husband. 'But tell me yours first.'

'Tomorrow we shall journey up to London, where I have secured two seats for the evening performance at the Savoy of Mr Gilbert and Mr Sullivan's new operetta *The Gondoliers*!'

'Oh, Samuel, that is so exciting!'

'And I am sure there will be time for us to include a visit to one or two of the museums in Kensington, and perhaps even take in Westminster Abbey.'

'Oh, Samuel, you are so wonderful,' said a happy Lucy, placing a kiss on her husband's cheek.

'You deserve every moment of it, my dear. If it was not for you, I don't believe that I would ever have solved the case. But now, tell me your surprise?'

'Well, I hope you will be pleasantly surprised,' said a smiling Lucy, coyly.

'You are teasing me, my love.'

'Yes, I suppose I am — but yes, I am sure you will be more than a little pleased when I tell you my news . . .'

POSTSCRIPT

The Templar's 'treasure' was reinterned inside the ancient tomb, which can be seen today in the village church of Meysey Hampton.

Robert Ross was buried next to his brother in a small village churchyard in Gloucestershire.

Many people still visit Tewkesbury Abbey today to view the ancient monuments — and some have even attempted — in vain — to understand the meaning of the strange letters on the outside of the tomb of Sir Roger de la Pole, the Templar Knight.

THE END

ALSO BY KERRY TOMBS

INSPECTOR RAVENSCROFT DETECTIVE MYSTERIES

Book 1: THE MALVERN MURDERS
Book 2: THE WORCESTER WHISPERERS
Book 3: THE LEDBURY LAMPLIGHTERS
Book 4: THE TEWKESBURY TOMB

FREE KINDLE BOOKS

Thank you for reading this book. If you enjoyed it please leave feedback on Amazon or Goodreads, and if there is anything we missed or you have a question about, then please get in touch. The author and publishing team appreciate your feedback and time reading this book.

We're very grateful to eagle-eyed readers who take the time to contact us. Please send any errors you find to corrections@joffebooks.com. We'll get them fixed ASAP.

Printed in Great Britain
by Amazon

57596162R00118